SHOW MODE

Raquel Rivera

ORCA BOOK PUBLISHERS

Library and Archives Canada Cataloguing in Publication

Rivera, Raquel, 1966–, author
Show mode / Raquel Rivera.
(Orca limelights)

Issued in print and electronic formats.
ISBN 978-1-4598-1204-8 (paperback).—ISBN 978-1-4598-1205-5 (pdf).—
ISBN 978-1-4598-1206-2 (epub)

I. Title. II. Series: Orca limelights
PS8635.I9435S56 2017   jc813'.6   c2016-904571-4
                    c2016-904572-2

First published in the United States, 2017
Library of Congress Control Number: 2016949058

Summary: In this high-interest novel for teen readers, Adina wants to
put together a perfect act for the school fashion show.

*Orca Book Publishers is dedicated to preserving the environment and has printed
this book on Forest Stewardship Council® certified paper.*

Orca Book Publishers gratefully acknowledges the support for
its publishing programs provided by the following agencies:
the Government of Canada through the Canada Book Fund and the Canada
Council for the Arts, and the Province of British Columbia through the BC
Arts Council and the Book Publishing Tax Credit.

Cover design by Rachel Page
Cover photography by Getty Images

ORCA BOOK PUBLISHERS
www.orcabook.com

Printed and bound in Canada.

20 19 18 17 • 4 3 2 1

*For the fun, spirited and dedicated students
and teachers of École FACE*

One

"*Gonna get, get, get down...*" We're all huddled around Seth's music player. Sandra's bobbing her head. It's a remix of "Bad Girls" by Gigamesh, Seth says. These days Seth is fully into disco. It *is* a nice jam.

We're planning our act for the fall fashion show. Finally! I've wanted to do Fashion Show for ages, but you have to be in ninth grade or higher to audition. Last year my older brother was in it. I was so jealous. They set up this cool runway, jutting off the school stage, especially for the show. Pop songs blare. It's nothing like our usual concerts, where we students play the music ourselves. In Fashion Show, we get to pick tunes, invent dances for them and make costumes—it's a lot of fun.

Our school is right downtown, so we could hold our meeting at any fast-food place or at the mall. But when the weather is warm like this, the lawns and big trees of the university quad are the best. At lunch hour, the seventh-graders like to play pickup soccer games here. But right now, after school, it's mostly college students and old people—professors—walking the paths from class to class, playing Frisbee or just lying on the slope, taking in the sun.

"And check this out. We can mix into—" Seth taps at his player, and Donna Summer starts crooning about how much love she's feeling over the *beep-beep* sound of a 1970s synthesizer.

This is too much for Sandra—she jumps up, even though the player isn't loud enough to really enjoy the music. She begins to move like a snake in a charmer's basket. She's got this ripple going, from the hem of her long purple dress to her chandelier earrings. That glint creeps across her face—a combination of mischief and joy—and her epic voice cuts loose, drowning out Donna. "*Oh, but it's good!*" she sings.

People walking by can't help looking. Mostly they're smiling. Some even groove along with

Sandra as they pass, and she grooves back. Sandra's voice is a gift, our singing teachers say. Think of Christina Aguilera, down low. Sandra sounds part opera, part Janis Joplin—and all herself. When Sandra sings, everybody notices.

She drops back down on the grass, blowing kisses to the people on the slope, who are whistling and cheering.

"Seth, baby, you know what I like!" Sandra wipes sweat off her face. It's too warm for long sleeves, but Sandra is quite overweight and she thinks she looks better when her curves are covered. "We're going to ace this audition, you guys."

I look around for Willow. The theme of our act will be backup singers, we decided. Now we need to choreograph our moves down the runway. If we nail it today, we can start practicing. Auditions are in just a few weeks, and to win a spot, the act's got to be really tight. "Willow—we need you!"

Her flute case is here, so she can't be far away. Willow goes nowhere without her flute. I scan the football field, then the pathways leading down to the traffic on Sherbrooke. Did she climb a tree?

"Willow!" By now Sandra and Seth are yelling too.

Willow emerges from the rock garden under the bridge. "You guys, there's the cutest squirrel back here. He ate all the leftovers in my lunchbox—from my hand."

"Ew." Sandra makes a face.

"You've got a bunch of twigs in your hair," Seth points out.

"We're plotting the walk—we need you!" I practically shout.

We have to choreograph moves that'll get us down the runway. Each act has up to six minutes to perform. Sandra and I have already worked out our storyline. We're backup singers who all want to be the lead. We each keep trying to sneak in front of the others, at different times. This allows for some nice switches in staging. Also, we can make it funny using slapstick stuff we learned in drama class, like the Keystone Cops or the Three Stooges (if we want to get violent about it). Whatever we do, we have to keep our moves simple and big, to communicate all the way to the back of the auditorium.

"Seth can spin Willow first," I suggest.

The spinning goes all right until they start traveling as if they're on the runway. They can't seem to manage. So Willow twirls herself while Seth walks beside her. It looks like he's turning her...sort of. People will probably get the idea. Meanwhile, Sandra and I are supposed to model-prance on either side. But it's impossible to prance as slowly as Seth and Willow are moving. And slow as they are, they still can't keep their hands touching.

"This isn't working," I say, but nobody hears me. They're all giggling at how stupid we look. Then Seth twirls Willow for real until she falls down. He whoops like a maniac and fakes a wrestling drop on her. Meanwhile, Willow's squealing her head off.

Sandra dumps handfuls of fallen leaves over them both. "Bravo, bravo!" she cries.

"Hey, guys—" I try again, but Sandra grabs me in a bear hug and lifts me off the ground, which she knows I hate.

"Get your sweaty hands off me." I twist and kick until she lets go.

"*Gawd*, all right." Sandra backs away. "It was just some fun."

Don't you hate it when people act all hurt, but they were the ones being obnoxious in the first place?

"We've only got a few weeks." I try to stay calm and reasonable, even though they're all acting like third-graders. "There's still a ton of stuff we have to—*quit it, Sandra!*"

Sandra's sprinkling leaves in my hair now, and I don't appreciate it. I'm not Willow, child of the forest.

"Will you relax, Adina?" Seth rolls onto his back, laughing up at me.

"It's not like we're getting graded on this," Willow adds. "Don't go turbo on us."

What have grades got to do with it? I'm the only one who's attended this school since kindergarten, so maybe they don't get it. I've been watching the high-school students put on Fashion Show for years. It's a huge deal. Hundreds of people—friends and family—pay good money to see it. The funds go to the graduating-class prom, so it's not a joke. Fashion Show is a professional-quality show—or as near as we can make it. That's not me going turbo or freaking out.

It's true Willow's parents have never taken her to Fashion Show, and Seth just joined the school last year. But Sandra should be jumping at this opportunity to show her talent. She *says* she wants to be the lead singer in a band.

But everyone's laughing, so I try to act like I don't mind. We've still got a few weeks to get things right.

Then my phone alarm goes off. Already? That means I have five minutes to run to the bus stop. If I miss this bus home, I'll have to wait ages for the next one.

"Saved by the bell." Sandra hurls herself down by the other leaf-covered idiots.

I grab my backpack, lunchbox and, of course, my violin case. "We have to decide our choreography soon," I tell them. "Because don't forget, there are also costumes to figure out," I shout, jogging backward toward Sherbrooke.

"Adina!" Willow's brushing at her head, like I should do the same. There's a clump of leaves poking out of my thick, curly, leaf-trap hair. I turn and run, plucking at my head. My backpack and violin case bump against me all the way down the block.

Two

Since I got into the school symphony orchestra, I'm supposed to practice *at least* an hour a day. We've been set seven pieces to learn for the next performance, but this concerto is my favorite by far. I admit, I spend most of my time playing this one. The melody always twists my heart, but in a good way. It's like a twinge that's almost painful, but I'm happy it's making me feel—if that makes any sense.

I know the piece, but I still use the sheet music. When we started learning music notation, back in first grade, it was like a game. By grade three I thought it was boring—learning how to read time signatures and what the black notes meant versus the white notes. But now I feel weird without it, even when I know the tune. Sheet music has become like a security blanket.

I lean forward and flip the page, and I'm in the difficult bit—quick bow work and a shift from first to fifth position. I play it over and over. I always feel calm and happy after playing this. Like how Mom says she feels after her meditation class.

Suddenly bhangra is blasting through the living room, practically blowing over my music stand. First the gunfire-fast drums. Then the strings come in. Finally, shrill vocals pierce my calm, happy brain. Dev must be home.

I knock on his bedroom door, but of course he can't hear. When I push it open, he starts madly clicking at the windows on his computer screen until he realizes I'm not Mom or Dad. Yeah, that's right, it's just me. He always pretends he's studying. "*Because this is his last year of high school. He knows he must keep top grades to be ready for pre-engineering next year,*" Mom likes to say.

But I know better. "Working hard?" I cross my arms and lean against the doorframe.

"What? Leave me alone, Adina." Not that I can hear him, but I'm pretty sure that's what he's saying. It's what he usually says to me. He turns back to his computer. Windows are popping open again.

"Turn down your music and I'm out of here," I promise. Dev is first French horn in our school's symphony orchestra, and he plays keyboards in the jazz band. But lately he's been on this Indian music kick. At home he's been listening to all Indian, all the time. I'm proud to be Indian— South Asian, whatever—but it's beginning to feel like I live in a Bollywood flick. Even though I know bhangra is not Bollywood. Dev has already explained that to me.

"Get out!" Dev twists around in his seat. He's glaring at me with buggy, outraged eyeballs. He seems mystified that I'm still in his room. He can be so dense.

"Turn down the freaking music!" I shout back. *Sheesh.* I used to think Dev was the greatest, but he's turning into a selfish *bleep*-hole.

I remember once when Mom was dashing between emptying Dev's lunchbox, pulling dinner things from the fridge and checking her laptop for last emails from work. I mentioned that I'd cleaned out my own lunchbox *and* emptied the dishwasher, and what did Dev do, again?

Mom stopped her whirling and gave me one of her serious looks. "*You and your brother have different lives, Adina—not better, not worse.*"

Why did I even bother even bringing it up? Mom is very big on not making comparisons. When I was little, every time I pointed out something unfair she'd say, "*You are younger,*" or "*You're a girl.*" Then, when I got old enough to figure out sexism and ageism, Mom switched her reasons. "*You're different people, is what I mean, Adina. My expectations of you and your brother are based on your unique personalities and capabilities.*" Which, when you think about it, is another way of saying Mom makes up random rules as she goes.

Like when I mentioned having emptied the dishwasher and ended up getting scolded. "*Concern yourself with your own efforts, Adina,*" she told me.

Most parents would be thrilled I'm doing well with the workload they give us at school. I have daily classes in voice and music, not to mention required credits in drama and visual art, as well as the usual academic subjects. Maybe Mom could notice that I *am* making an effort.

Meanwhile, Dev only comes out of his room for meals, with the attitude that he's doing the rest of us a favor. He's so inconsiderate. Like right now. As if I would be anywhere near his smelly room if he wasn't screeching music all over the house.

"Headphones!" I point at the fat, cushiony headphones he got for Diwali last year. I frantically mime putting them over my ears.

For a moment he actually focuses. He turns down his music. "You've got junk in your hair." He's looking at me as if I'm roadkill—equal parts disgusting and pathetic.

What, *more* leaf bits? I pat my head and find a poking stem. I try to untangle it.

Dev snarls, "Don't do that here." He reaches for his headphones and turns his back on me.

Don't you hate it when everyone acts like a total pain? Stupid brother. Infuriating friends.

I'm still pulling at that leaf stem as I slam the door and stomp back to my violin. The strings buzz when I start playing. I have to force myself to lighten my bow stroke.

Three

I bump into Seth coming out of music class. Basic woodwind is next door to advanced strings. We both have math next, so together we dart through the sea of students coming and going. Seth leads, swinging his clarinet case to clear a path out of the music department. I don't know why, but clarinet seems to be the choice of kids who don't care about playing an instrument. Like Seth, for example. He wants to be a DJ—he wants to mix. Seth says *the music* is his true instrument.

He smashes though the fire doors, and we're in the north wing hallway. Math class is in the south wing, four floors above. We pass the girls' bathroom and are moving full speed across the marble floors of the great front hall.

Chatter from the north wing fades behind us. Dusty sunlight streams through the old-fashioned, glass-paneled front doors. Coming our way is a slow-moving kindergarten snake. Pairs of stubby kids, holding hands, are surrounded by shushing teachers. I spot my little reading partner and high-five him as we pass. (This semester, Reading Partners is part of our Ethics and Citizenship class.)

We push hard against the south-stairwell doors, booting it up the nearest staircase. The south-wing stairwell actually has two sets of stairs twisting around each other, like a double helix or an M.C. Escher drawing. The dingy glass walls allow you to see the other set of stairs, but you have to wait until the next floor if you want to change over. Maybe when the school was originally built ages ago, one was for going up and one for coming down. Now we just pick the one that's less clogged.

Above me, Seth turns to speak—I dodge his backpack before it smashes my face. "Give me your notes? I have to copy."

"What, again?" I don't know how Seth keeps up in math, since he's mostly copying my homework. But he aces the tests.

By the time I've got my backpack unzipped, found my math binder and kept my pencil case from flying all over the place, we're almost at the classroom. I'm hot, and my hair's coming undone. I have to blow it out of my eyes, since my hands are full of dismantled school junk. So annoying. Seth doesn't bother with homework, so how is it *I'm* the one scrambling at the last minute? That's just wrong.

I move over to the wall, drop my bag and hand him the stupid binder. He must know I'm upset because he's slouching over me, shuffling around, trying to catch my eye. He smooths my hair away and tells me, "I finished the mix. Our music is ready."

Our music is ready? My sweaty frustration evaporates. It feels like a bright light is flooding through me. It's good news. But maybe not as good as Seth touching my face.

Either way, I forgive him completely.

Our music is ready! This means we can finally nail down our dance moves. I already asked our science teacher if we could use his room for practice at lunch periods. He's a very approachable person. There are many teachers with big classrooms, but mostly—without going into gory details—it's wiser to just slink to your desk and escape as soon as class is finished.

But our science teacher told me practicing in his room was absolutely no problem. Any lunch hour we wanted, he said. Well, now we want! I'm going to tell him as soon as math is over.

Seth takes the binder that I'm still holding in midair. He picks up my backpack too, which is a nice gesture, if you think about it. We go into class, the final bell clanging around us.

Four

"It's my fault. I didn't realize you were in different acts." Our science teacher is at his desk, peering at the bunch of us. He pushes up his glasses, looking from our group to the other. "I seem to have double-booked my room."

"That's okay—we can squeeze in." Dawn smiles. She's one of the girls in the other act. They're in Dev's class. I secretly call these three the Prima Donnas—after Dawn, get it? And also because they *are* perfect. They're pretty, popular and invent great acts.

Every year the Prima Donnas have performed an act in Fashion Show. They outstyle pretty much everyone else. Last year Dev played the role of cool jazz cat in their act. They got him this fedora, which he tilted over one eye.

The Prima Donnas dressed up like 1920s flappers, shimmying in their fringe dresses, while Dev waved around a borrowed trumpet. It was kind of sexy but with funny moments—like when Dev accidentally blared the trumpet in Dawn's face. Dawn did this hilarious stagger-dance, weaving down the runway.

I think Dev and Dawn were going together at the time, but Dev wouldn't spill. Anyway, it's likely that Dev has gone with pretty much every girl in his grade at some point. They like his dark eyes and floppy hair. Obviously, they don't have to see him first thing in the morning, scratching his bed head and other parts, which I will spare you by not mentioning. Let's just say it's not a good look. Yeah, Dev owes his love life to hair products.

"Both groups practice in here?" Prima Donna Jill looks around, eyebrows rising. She laughs. "You guys haven't seen my brother dance yet. Elephant, much?"

In a gesture of brotherly love, Seth does a slow-motion roundhouse kick at Jill's butt, and she bats it away like she's done it a million times.

Prima Donna Sofia is the only real dancer among us. She studies ballet, and it shows—she's got amazing posture. Sofia is probably the reason the Prima Donnas' moves are always so good in the fashion show. "But seriously," she says, "if you guys want to use this space, we can practice in the hall. Then maybe switch halfway..."

"It's okay—I know another place." Seth hoists his backpack and turns to us. "Follow me." Spinning on his sneakers, he takes off.

Sandra, Willow and I pound down the stairs after him. He's taking them two at a time. In this school you become a stair master pretty fast. Instrument cases, heavy backpacks and five flights of stairs—I guess it makes up for our puny phys-ed program.

Seth slows when he hits the basement level. We follow him through the old halls. The school building is more than a hundred years old. I remember this whenever I'm in the basement. With all these arched tunnels and turns, it looks like a medieval dungeon with a paint job. We move past the big gym and dozens of locked rooms. By this time, we all know where Seth is headed. He creaks open the door to the Sub Theater.

The gloomy Sub Theater is a black-painted performance space that used to be a swimming pool.

This was ages ago, when students wore pinafores and boater hats. Back then a kid drowned, and they emptied the pool forever.

"We're probably not supposed to be here," muses Willow.

"Nobody's ever explicitly said, so we're not *not* supposed to be here," Sandra reasons. Meanwhile, the door slams behind us.

On account of the black walls and no windows, we are in total darkness. There's a massive lighting system for jazz-band concerts and plays, but it's controlled from the booth behind the seats. There must be an ordinary wall switch in here somewhere. "Ow!" I smack my shin against the metal frame that holds the seating tiers together. So at least I know where I am.

"You okay, Adina?" Willow's high voice sounds creepy in the dark.

"Where's the door gone?" Seth says.

"Someone prop it open until we find the light," Sandra calls out.

"My leg freaking *hurts*," I say. It really does, but I'm laughing because this is so stupid.

Then my laugh catches in my throat. Something is brushing across my face. I freeze—except for my heart, which is pounding so hard it feels like it's coming out my ears.

It's a hand! There's a cold hand on my face!

"Oops, sorry." Seth is giggling in my ear. "I've got something here—" His textbook-stuffed backpack thuds to the floor, landing on my foot.

"*Yow!*" I collapse against him, and he holds me up. He can barely speak, he's laughing so hard.

"The zipper is stuck—" He eases me down to the floor as I'm moaning and laughing. I can hear Willow and Sandra shrieking, so they're probably smashing into each other too. We could all be murdered down here and no one would hear us.

As that thought starts creeping up my spine, a light pops on—right under Seth's face. I can't help screaming because he looks like a total ghoul.

It looks cool, actually. He's shining a little flashlight under his chin.

Then Sandra's got the door open, and light filters in. Seth is casting his beam around, and he pulls out three more flashlights. "I thought these would be perfect for the act. Check it out— microphones for the backup singers!" he announces. "These are military grade. Small but powerful."

"You got these from your uncle?" Willow asks. Seth nods. His uncle is in the armed forces.

Seth shows how these will make good props and add lighting effects to the act. He tosses, gestures and, of course, sings into the flashlight like it's a microphone. This last bit transforms his face. Under stage lights it will look even better. *Yes!* It's a brilliant idea. It will really make the act stand out. With the mics in our hands, we seem to gesture naturally, as if we are backup singers for real.

Seth pulls mini-speakers from his backpack and plugs in his player. We start our routine with two of us in front and two behind, all doing hip twitches in sync. The funky intro on the Gigamesh remix *demands* attitude. Even low-key Willow is giving off a supermodel vibe.

We move forward, stop, bop, then step forward again. When the vocals come in, we backup singers start to lose our cool. First we fan, four across. I suggest a move I saw on YouTube— a front-back step with raised arms, like we're a choir singing "Hallelujah."

"We should all clap once, right here"—Sandra demonstrates—"when there's clapping in the tune." We run through it a few times. We keep the moves sharp and tight, the same as the keyboards in the song. It looks good. When Seth's mix goes into the next song, everyone agrees that he should be the first to try cutting in front, grabbing the lead-singer position.

He steps out, flashlight under his face. He does some spins and locking, pretending he's all Bruno Mars and Michael Jackson and whatnot, lip-synching into the flashlight. He looks hot.

Then I remember the rest of us are supposed to be acting annoyed, so I say, "What if we take big steps, like we want to crush Seth—we have to keep moving forward, right? And he turns to us, taking big steps backward, as if he's scared?"

Willow says, "I like how the vocals start singing about love right at that moment."

"We should ham it up," Sandra adds. "Seth, you lip-synch the lyric to us."

Seth mimes a sappy crooner.

"Yeah, like that!" she cries. "And we pull at you, to get you back in line with the rest of us."

Everyone is laughing while Willow cues the music again. This is so good—we're going to get a spot in Fashion Show for sure! I suggest that when we three are pulling Seth back, we switch on our flashlights too and swing them in angry, random directions.

"Yeah!" Everyone agrees.

The ideas keep coming, each new move bursting from the one before. This is the most productive meeting we've had yet.

Don't you love it when things finally start to flow?

Five

Oh no. Who knew there would be so many acts practicing for the audition?

The big gym looks as jammed as during Science Fair. Seth is freaked out too, I can tell. His eyes are popping. It's a few steps down to the gym floor, so from this level we are looking over a sea of room dividers, set up to create practice spaces. Supposedly, we can all work in privacy this way, but I can see what everyone is doing.

I feel Sandra's hand on my shoulder. "It's too cold out in the quad," she says. She must know what I'm thinking—that even if teachers are sick of being pestered for their classrooms, there must be a better place to practice than this.

"I don't like it," I mutter as we head to our assigned space.

Willow says, "I think it's kind of interesting." She's rubbernecking through the aisles, peering into each practice stall with a goofy smile on her face.

"Don't look," I hiss. "People will think we're trying to steal ideas." Actually, what's more troubling is that people can now steal *our* moves. I breathe a bit easier when I see that our space is the last on a row. There's no excuse for anyone to pass by unless they're prepared to be obvious about snooping.

Seth sets up the music. The big sign on the board tells everyone to keep their volume to an absolute minimum or risk losing their space. Meanwhile, Sandra and I try to coach Willow. She needs to sass up her moves when she's in front. We discussed this privately already. We don't want to make Willow feel bad, but we've been practicing for a while now, and she still doesn't seem to be finding her character.

The key, our drama teacher says, is to look inside ourselves. It's not about spouting dialogue or, in this case, executing moves. Actors have to know background stuff about their characters even if it doesn't appear directly in the show.

Maybe they were orphans raised by drunken uncles, or they have an allergy to peanuts. Creating this background helps *inform* the choices actors make as they play a role, our drama teacher says. I like that. It's like doing homework. So long as you prepare, you'll be ready for whatever the test—or the show—throws at you.

I decided my character is from a tremendously rich family. She's doing this on a whim. This makes her moves cool, not peppy or bouncy. Sandra sees her character as a desperately talented singer who's never happy unless she's in the spotlight. When she shoves her way to the front, she makes her gestures bigger, more radiant, than when she's stuck in the back.

Meanwhile, Willow looks like she's just blocking out her moves. She hasn't gotten into the spirit of anyone.

We ask her what she imagines when she's doing her routine.

Willow looks bewildered.

"Is there any feeling, or mood, that comes to you?" I say.

Her eyebrows rise higher. "I'm doing the steps. I'm keeping time."

Sandra and I perform her part, showing different ways she might put more expression into her movement. Willow applauds and nods, but it doesn't really change her own attempts.

"Moving on!" Seth cries. "You guys are boring." He starts the music, and we hustle into position.

We start foursquare, then fan out. Seth moves to the front, swiveling and locking through his routine while we advance on him. Then Willow boots him back in line with a high kick. See, right there she could really work that move, but she doesn't. We advance again, and then it's my turn to scramble up front.

This is the instrumental bit of the song. The vocals have faded out and the keyboards are rocking the main riff. Then a beat comes in—more synthesizer. I shine my flashlight around.

I'm pretty happy with my part. Mom and I have a kind of tradition where we learn the dance routines in our favorite Bollywood movies. It's something she and her cousins did growing up, and I guess she passed it on to me. So now I'm pretending I'm kicking sand, like Madhuri Dixit in *Lajja*, until the *sh-sh* sound of the hi-hat starts up. Then I go into a classic disco move, The Sprinkler. (Thanks, YouTube.) One hand is behind my head, the other straight out. My flashlight is shooting rays—sprays—in little jolts across the audience. When the bridge fades to the next verse, Donna Summer comes in, sighing, "*You get me—ooh—*" and I sashay back to the line, trying to emote reluctance while lip-synching into the flashlight.

Then the worst happens. We're being watched.

The Prima Donnas are checking us out, hips tilted, arms crossed under their perfect chests. How long have they been here? Sandra is starting her routine. The Prima Donnas must learn no more!

"Stop!" I cry out. Willow, Seth and Sandra turn. They must hear the panic in my voice. "Quit spying!" I shout at the Donnas before I know it.

Suddenly they're on orange alert—high risk, all forces ready for combat. Dawn, Jill and Sofia shift and sway, their faces snarly and sour. I step back.

I don't know what got into me, shouting at them like that. No one in their right mind goes up against the Donnas. I feel woozy. The gym floor beckons, but somehow I manage not to collapse in a heap.

"*Spying*?" Dawn sneers. "What for? You losers are a mess."

Jill puts her hands on her hips and leans forward like she's sharing a secret. "You're all over the place. We couldn't see what's going on even if we wanted to."

Sofia just nods, but her superior expression is saying, *You guys are sick, and not in the good way*. I can feel my shoulders sag as Dawn starts in again, pointing at Willow.

"Space Case looks like she's moving through mud, and Chunkmeister"—her finger pivots toward Sandra—"needs more time to get to the front. She runs like a duck."

"Yeah." Jill and Sofia are the perfect chorus.

All this time, a fuzzy black has been closing in on my vision, until I'm peering through a small hole. Now Seth steps into the circle, and I can see him too.

"You shouldn't talk!" His face is flushed. I've never seen him so indignant, not even when his phone got smashed in a game of keep-away. "I've seen your act—those stiff arms and legs? Some ugly!"

Jill screeches. "You little fink—I told you to stay clear of the rec room!"

I blink, and my circle of vision gets wider. I guess Seth has been doing spying of his own, at home.

"We were just working up ideas," Sofia adds. "Obviously, you have no clue about choreography."

"We're wasting our time." Dawn turns away, and the others follow. "We were just wondering how you kiddies were doing. Sorry to say, but get ready to look up, waaay up."

Sofia and Jill laugh, hair tossing over their shoulders. "Yeah—we'll be on the runway, as always. You'll be watching from the seats."

* * *

There are no chairs in the practice space, so we're on the floor. No one feels like finishing the act. I reach into my backpack to get my sweater. I can't seem to stop shivering.

Sandra looks miserable. Willow's comforting arm hugs Sandra's shoulders. It was that Chunkmeister comment. I silently curse Dawn. Sandra is sensitive about her weight, which you wouldn't think, because she comes off as a really strong person. Most days she is. She's got style, and she's always laughing. People like her, even if she doesn't let them get too close. Most days she knows all this. And then the perfect Donnas have to throw her weight in her face.

"They're just being little witches," I tell her. "They're trying to psych us out—they're afraid of the competition." It could be true. And besides, we need Sandra feeling confident if the act is going to work.

Willow looks at me, jaw dropped in outrage. "Adina, what they did was bullying." She stands up, brushing floor crud off her butt. "I'm going to report them—right now."

Huh? Report *what*, exactly? Don't you hate it when people overreact?

"Don't report it," I hiss at her. "It'll be a whole thing!"

We'd have to wait for ages to see the vice-principal—and honestly, what would we say?

Sure, Dawn was mean. But everyone's mean sometimes. Sandra regularly calls Seth a fool, for example, and Willow doesn't go ballistic. Also, Dawn didn't single out Sandra. *That* would be bullying, right? She was equal-opportunity dumping on the whole act.

"We don't have a lot of time." I've said this so often, it's like my new motto. But I seem to be the only one keeping track. I hold on to Willow so she doesn't rush off, making this one of her random causes for justice. We should keep our focus on the act.

Then, even as I'm speaking, an uncomfortable thought pops into my head. Some of the Donnas' criticisms may have been a teensy bit correct. We might need to make changes.

"Maybe if we cut out the little extras," Seth mutters. He's thinking the same thing. "Maybe our transitions are too complicated..."

"We could simplify the line moves when one of us is in front," I add. "That will make it easier too..."

"You guys!" Willow is glaring at us. "What they said about Sandra—we have to tell."

Please, no. Let's not make this more than it is. Willow didn't even notice the Space-Case comment, which proves that Dawn's remarks weren't all that hurtful. I turn to Sandra. She definitely looks unsure about Willow's plan. Of course she does. If I were in her place, I'd want to forget this and move on.

"Sandra doesn't want to report it," I tell Willow. "Let's focus on perfecting the act. Sandra can show them with her finale—she's going to be great. This is a minor setback. We shouldn't dwell. Show business isn't for wimps. Right, Sandra?"

Sandra's mouth is drooping, twitching a little, but she's nodding agreement. She probably knows she's going to feel worse if the school gets involved.

"Thank you!" I take a deep breath. "We have more important things to deal with, right?" Willow must see that it's not a big deal—not really.

But Willow is gathering her things. She's wrestling with her jacket like it's fighting back. Her legs buckle as she shifts her backpack. She's got that stubborn, storm-cloud look on her face. Willow never argues. She's a force of nature instead.

"Where are you going? We have to rehearse," I say.

Seth adds, "My sister's friends are a drag—
I know. But we can't let them get to us."

"Willow, seriously, I'm okay." Sandra's mouth
has stopped twitching.

But Willow marches off, her instrument case
cradled in her arms. "Yeah right, I have to rehearse,"
she calls back. "I've got my flute to practice."

Six

S eth starts packing up his mini-speakers. We're obviously not rehearsing anymore. If the Donnas meant to sabotage us, they couldn't have done a better job. Looking at Sandra, somehow I feel guilty. But Dawn was the one being mean. And then Willow got all dramatic, so now Sandra feels even worse.

"We could get material for the costumes," Seth suggests. "My mom gave me her Fabric Plus member card."

"Yes!" I want to kiss him. That's just what we need—a shopping trip! "Sandra, let's do it. We'll get something really disco queen." I put my arms around her, but she shrugs me off.

"You guys go. I have stuff to do." She loops

her pink fun-fur scarf around her neck. It catches on the stuffed spikes that jut from her backpack.

"But we totally need your opinion," I say, but Sandra won't look up. Is she mad at me?

She gives us both a little smile and says, "I trust you guys. Go for glamor—go fabulous. Do like me, and you'll do fine." She sounds her usual self. I wish she'd look me in the eye, but I'm probably being overly sensitive. Willow must be rubbing off on me.

*   *   *

It isn't until Seth and I get to Plaza Saint-Hubert that I realize it's just the two of us—almost like a date. We take our time walking to Seth's mom's favorite fabric shop. Saint-Hubert is filled with formal dress shops, and the window displays are good costume inspiration.

Then we stop into the games store, because Seth needs to buy some kind of voucher card. He looks so cute and excited staring at the stupid thing that I can't help grabbing it from him. I dash out the shop door.

He chases me around the clothing racks on the sidewalk until I let him catch me. He has to grab me with both arms because I'm trying to hide the card inside my jacket. But I can tell he doesn't really mind. And I'm laughing like crazy, because he's tickling me.

I can feel his breath against my ear as I give up the card. "Let's get a frozen smoothie," he says.

Normally I'd say it's too cold for frozen smoothies, but right now I don't feel cold at all. "Let's get coconut," I agree.

When we arrive at Fabric Plus, we head straight for the remnants bin. "Check this." Seth is laughing at a bundle of vomit-green polyester. "Hey, my sister should get it—they're doing a Franken-monster theme."

I pull out a big square of black satin. I wear it like a cape, with two corners tied around my neck. I imagine I'm Black Widow. Not the lame Black Widow of the *Avengers* movie, but the original, in Dev's vintage comic collection. Her name is Claire Voyant. She kills evildoers and sends them down to Satan's lair.

But okay—get focused. Costumes, Fashion Show. What kind of fabric do we need? I sink my arms elbow deep into the remnants. I feel the slip of satin, the nubble of tweed, the grain of canvas.

"These pieces are too small. We'll have to look at the real fabric." I sigh and untie my cape, putting it back on the pile. "It's too bad. I like the shine of this one."

"The shiny stuff is kept over here," Seth says.

The shop is full of twists and turns, but Seth leads me as if he's an expert on the place. He's been coming here since he was tiny, because his mom is a sewing maniac.

This is maybe why the shop lady was so friendly when we came in. She doesn't seem bothered by us wandering around either. Don't you hate it when storekeepers wig out just because you're young? It's like they assume you're going to make a mess or rob them or something. We pass a ribbon display and turn into a small nook.

"Wow!" I exclaim. When Seth promised shiny, he was not joking. Roll upon roll of fabric is here, in rich, royal colors. There's scarlet, crimson, robin's-egg blue. There's purple, of course, and gold. Some fabrics are smooth, and some have sequins. Seth is smiling proudly, like he made them himself.

"What do you like? I like the smooth," I chatter. "See how it glints in the light? How much is this? Which color is best?"

Seth starts pulling out rolls as I touch them. We have to keep costs low, so silk and rayon are out. Eventually I choose a flame orange, a rich blue and the gold.

"You'd look beautiful in all those colors," Seth says.

I glance at him. Does he realize he's being nice? He seems busy with the fabric. Suddenly I feel nervous. I can't think, and I have an important decision to make about colors.

"Gold then," is what my mouth says. Seth heaves the roll over to the big table for cutting.

From my school agenda, I rip out the page with our scribbled measurements. I hand it to the shop lady, who helps us figure out how much we need. She unrolls the slithery, shimmery fabric. She doesn't even snip with the scissors, just holds them open and pushes through. I reach for the gorgeous, golden folds and make them ripple.

"You want to wear it now," the lady says with a chuckle, and Seth drapes it over my shoulders.

In all this gold, I feel like a queen—a true disco queen.

Then I remember Willow and Sandra. I haven't even thought about them since we left the school, I guess because Seth and I are having so much fun. "You think the others will like this fabric?" I ask.

"Sure, why not?" Seth says.

He doesn't get it. He couldn't care less about this stuff. I smooth my gold-covered arms. I'll text them a photo right away—that should get them excited about the act again.

Seth picks up the trailing end of our fabric and wraps it over my head and around. I start giggling because I must look ridiculous. Even the store lady is laughing at us.

"Very nice, your girlfriend, very pretty," she tells Seth. I get busy untangling myself from the fabric, waiting to hear him say we're just friends. He doesn't say a thing.

Seven

I scoop up the potato gravy with Mom's freshly made puri bread—a crispy-licious little pillow that deflates in my mouth. I must have gobbled the first ones too fast, because I have to sit back and stretch my stomach. I burp with my mouth closed, so no one notices. I drink some water. Mom never lets us have soda pop with dinner.

Dev is lost in a vintage *Avengers* comic on his iPad. Our parents always let us read at the dinner table—they like us to read. When we were little, Dad tried to encourage us by reading out loud at the table while we ate. But he never chose anything remotely interesting, like one of my picture books or Dev's *Captain Underpants* series. No, Dad would drone from his newspaper or a software magazine until Dev and I rushed to our rooms for something better to bring back to the table.

Actually, now that I think of it, there was always a little smile on Dad's face when this happened. Then he'd say, "*What, this story is no good either? Oh well. Suit yourselves.*"

Dad reaches for another puri from the oil-stained paper towel. He's reading, but it's my Early Progress Report from school. Mom plunked it on the table when she brought in the first round of puris. Now she's finally sitting to eat too, but I can tell she's dying to discuss my report.

Does anyone have a normal family that has real conversations over dinner? That must be nice. I get up to refill the gravy bowl, and Mom nods her thanks. We usually eat pretty late because Mom insists we all eat proper, home-cooked meals. But her work as an architect keeps her busy too. I lean back against my chair—an Eames, Mom calls it, which is some design she's proud of owning. I have to say, it *is* the most comfortable dining chair of any in my friends' homes, so I guess Mom does know something.

"You've been letting this fashion-show nonsense get out of hand." She wags the gravy spoon at me. Dad looks up from the report.

"You will stay home this weekend and think about how you can do better." He breaks his stern gaze and turns to Mom. "So tasty, the bhaji, as always," he murmurs. She fluffs like a little bird. I sigh. Why can't they be nice to me?

Dad is all about grounding. It's his single parenting tool. I'm just lucky he can't be bothered to follow through. His record is one full week, but that was when Dev thought his horn had been stolen. The school tries to keep security tight, but musical instruments are hot property, worth hundreds of dollars. Students and parents have to sign a responsibility slip every year to use the school's instruments. Luckily, it turned out that Dev's French horn wasn't stolen. The janitor had found Dev's horn case and brought it to the music department for safekeeping. Dad said Dev was still grounded for leaving it unattended.

Now I'm supposedly grounded for the whole weekend—just for missing a science project. "It's not even an official report card," I tell them. My progress reports have always shown a long column of Ss, for "satisfactory," in all my subjects. Just this once in my entire life I get a single N for "needs work," and Mom and Dad go ape.

"This is a very bad sign, Adina," Mom says. Dad may be finished with me, but she's just warming up. "You should be getting serious about your studies. You know that next year's grades are vital for applying to colleges." Whenever she talks about school, Mom's accent goes super Hindi. She starts switching her *v*'s and *w*'s. It's so annoying. I grab another puri from the pile, add a dollop of potato bhaji and stuff it into my mouth.

Dev looks up from his comic. He *loves* it when I get in trouble. He puts on this ultra-phony, concerned expression. Mom and Dad are clueless if they can't hear how fake suck-up he's being when he says, "Mom's right, Adina. Your studies are very important." His eyelids drop, and he nods slowly, like he has much wisdom to offer. I wonder how much of this spicy bhaji I could shove up his nose before he started hitting back.

But okay, that science project *was* a mess-up on my part. This never happens to me.

I remember when I found out about it. We had been horsing around in science class, waiting for the teacher to fix the Smart board so he could show a movie about pollution. Our noise must've been getting on his nerves, because he started yelling through his cords and cables that we should review our assignments. Then he said he was sure no one needed reminding that they were due that day.

Assignment? I'd looked around. Everyone else was rooting through their bags as if they knew what he was talking about. What assignment?

I poked Willow, sitting next to me. I gave her the *what's going on*? bug-eyed look. She gave me the *don't be an idiot* frown, waving her assignment paper in my face. As she checked her work, finger running across the page line by line, I read over her shoulder.

When were we assigned this? And where had I been at the time?

I'd started to scribble down everything I could remember about the topic—lithosphere, hydrosphere...don't ask. Obviously, it wouldn't be my best work, but I'd pull in a grade higher than zero. Then the lights switched off for the movie. My last chance was gone.

Now, at the dinner table, Dev's still being a jackass, loving my pain. I guess I'm better entertainment than Claire Voyant and the other Avengers.

I know better than to tell them why I forgot about the assignment. It was on the same page as the measurements, which I ripped out and gave to the fabric-store lady. That would completely set Mom against Fashion Show. She might even forbid me to do it. I erase the whole thought from my head, in case she reads my mind. But she's too busy talking.

"...can't be allowed to interfere with your regular schoolwork. Fashion Show is not a priority—your music also must come before. Are you listening?"

"Yes, Mom. Of course." I tell her I know I made a mistake. I promise to hand in all assignments for the rest of the year. "I'll think about what you said." It always makes Mom happy when I promise to think. She gives one firm nod and the subject is closed. Dev looks disappointed but goes back to his comic.

And I *will* think about it. I think I'll turn into Black Widow, catch criminals and send them to hell before I ever give up our act for the fashion show.

Eight

S inging class can be stressful because our teachers are really strict. They don't seem to believe in positive reinforcement or the importance of self-esteem. They're more interested in pointing out our faults.

Maybe they're mean because they are so heavily outnumbered by us. Most of the time, we ninth-graders take our classes in smaller groups. And in music, of course, we're all studying different instruments. We go to woodwind, brass, strings or percussion, depending. Choir is the only thing we all do together.

So even though there are four singing teachers down on the floor—one for each section of the choir—we kids are about a hundred strong. We stand on rising steps that line the walls.

The teachers are surrounded. We could create a serious stampede if we ever decided to, I don't know, *revolt* or something. I can see us all screaming, "*Liberty! Fraternity!*" as we rush down in a great swoop, music binders held high. Not that we've ever come close to doing that. Mostly we just do what they say.

Today we've got a new song. It's the first chorus from *Te Deum*, by Charpentier. The lyrics are in Latin, which is easier to remember than you might think—easier than the German songs, for example. Plus, there aren't that many words. The trick is to remember what phrase is coming up next and how many times we have to repeat it. I Google-translated the lyrics, thinking maybe the story would help me remember, but there's no story at all. It's a whole bunch of praises, about heaven and Earth, some glorious choir, as well as prophets and martyrs. Charpentier was quite religious. When we get it right, the song does have a very rousing effect. It's kind of like we're a bunch of trumpeting angels coming down and saying, "*Hey! Check all this majesty, you worms!*"

Sandra is breathing over my music because she forgot hers. We're together in the alto section.

Actually, Sandra could be in alto or soprano, but she's in alto because there are fewer of us. Willow is over in soprano. And last week Seth got shifted out of tenor on account of his new low voice.

We often share sheet music, but today Sandra's being a pain about it. She keeps pulling it toward her, blocking our next line. It's my music, after all—I'm the one doing the favor.

"...*majestatis gloriae tuae*..." She's ignoring my looks, so I give the paper a sharp tug in my direction. Then, while the tenor teacher is telling off his section of the choir, Sandra breaks the main rule of singing class. She speaks.

"Quit hogging it," she hisses in my ear.

"You're being the hog," I spit back.

Suddenly, just when I most want to give her a sharp pinch, Sandra goes all teary-eyed. "Are you talking about my weight?"

What? Sandra and I have been friends since kindergarten. She's always been big. I couldn't care less about her size.

Is Dawn's dumb comment still bugging her? *I* never called her Chunkmeister, so why give *me* grief? As I'm staring at her, her face changes from tragic to sly. The alto teacher's sharp voice shoots up through the choir.

"Absolutely no talking!" she calls. "You know the rule. Sandra, Adina, you each must sing for us—alone!"

Everyone stops and turns. The tenors look happy they're not getting yelled at anymore. I want to disappear. This has never happened to me. Don't you hate being in trouble? It's so undignified. And worse—way worse—my singing voice is not that strong, not like Sandra's. I feel faint, as if my head is leaving my body. Luckily, we're in the highest row, so I can lean back against the wall and catch my breath.

"We'll give Adina a minute to compose herself," the teacher announces. Everyone's looking at me. "Sandra, you can sing the line first. From the top, please."

But that's not fair—Sandra loves showing off! I'm the only one getting punished here.

That's when it dawns on me that Sandra has set me up. Would she do that? She knows how I feel about my singing voice. I never do extra-curricular singing activities—not any of the a capella groups, not the girls' jazz choir, nothing. Wow, she must be really mad at me. But why?

If I think about this right now, I'll lose it. I have to get myself together.

"*Pleni sunt caeli et terra*," Sandra bellows with gusto.

I don't have much time. I take calming breaths. Breathing is key in singing. I close my eyes. I remember Mom showing me her meditation breathing. I ignore the murmurs of appreciation rippling through the class—*la diva* has finished. It's my turn already. I try to slow my thumping heart.

I open my eyes and rip the music—*my* music—from Sandra's fingers. I make a silent vow to never, ever lend her my music again. I look straight ahead, through the little window above the classroom door. On this row, the window is at eye level, so I can see into the hall. I imagine I'm out there, all by myself. I don't see the heads of the students below me. I don't see the teachers, tapping their fingers and waiting. And mostly, I do *not* see the betrayer next to me.

"*Pleni*—uh—hmn—sorry." My throat catches. I cough and start again.

"*Pleni sunt caeli et terra...*" As I warble, I imagine Sandra toppling down the rows of the ninth-grade choir like a bowling ball, smashing through the teachers below like they're pins. "*...majestatis gloriae tuae...*" I imagine Sandra, bruised and red-faced, arms and legs flailing among the scolding teachers. "*...Te gloriosus Apostolorum chorus.*"

Nine

At lunch hour, I rush off by myself. Staring into shop windows at the Eaton Centre, I have to brush away tears. How can I ever face singing class again? What a pathetic dork I must have seemed, yelping and chirping in front of the entire choir. *Thanks for that, Sandra.* But then my nose catches the smells wafting from Pizza Dolce Vita, and I realize I'm starving. Lucky I have cash on me.

Have you noticed how everything seems less dire after a fresh, hot pizza slice? You know how the green pepper is still a touch crisp when you bite into it, and the cheese oozes with tomatoey goodness?

Sandra and I can always talk out our differences. She probably has no idea how upset she made me today.

* * *

"Hey, guys, wait for me!"

I catch up with Sandra and Willow on the school steps. There are still a few minutes before the bell rings, so it's pretty much mayhem around us. Crowds of kids are milling in the courtyard, rushing in and out the doors, making them swing and slam. A football flies back and forth over everyone's heads.

"That was some burn you pulled on me." I fake-punch Sandra on the arm, trying for a tone of friendly complaint. "What's up with that?"

I don't know what I'm expecting. That she might apologize, I guess. That she might say she wasn't thinking, or she was in a bad mood over something else. I guess I'm hoping for anything that'll make me feel better—make me recognize my friend again. Instead, I get a blank look that says, *What burn? What are you talking about?*

I look over at Willow. She was in singing class too—she knows what I mean, right?

Willow's eyes have gone all big and shiny, like when she's gazing on a dear little animal creature and her heart is melting with love.

"You sounded good today, Adina. You muffed the first notes, but you pulled it together. You have no reason to be ashamed."

Nope, she doesn't know what I mean.

I feel the bump and slide of bodies squeezing past me on the steps. I steady myself against the railing, leaning into Sandra.

"It's no big deal, Adina." Sandra brushes me off. "Don't be so sensitive. You're the one who says show business isn't for wimps."

I guess I am. Somehow that doesn't make me feel better.

The first bell goes, and my friends head in. I tell them I've forgotten something. I'll be there in a minute. The crowds are moving inside. I duck out of the way, under the railing, and sit, dangling my legs over the edge of the steps. I just need a second to think. Did I get it wrong? I remember the look on Sandra's face before we were caught talking. She meant to get me in trouble. Or am I being a suck?

Then I feel a sharp jab on my head—"Ow!"— and a football lands in my lap.

What the—?

The football owners are laughing. One of them has his hand over his mouth in apologetic shock. Another is doubled over with laughter, and the third is frantically waving that I should toss it back to him. "Pass it!" he shouts.

If I had a penknife on me right now, this football would be a flat mess.

I tuck it under my arm and crawl back under the railing, acting like I'm taking their football into school with me.

"Hey!" Impatient Dude shouts again, so I turn around. The second bell goes. I don't need his stupid ball anyway. I hurl it, trying to drive its pointy end into his face the way he did to me. But I can't throw for beans, and it falls short.

I storm inside to the sounds of hooting laughter.

Ten

The sewing room is on the top floor of Seth's house, tucked under the slanted roof. A round window peeks onto the quiet street below. Seth's mom has an elaborate present-wrapping station in here too. I guess once you get started with all those little drawers and compartments for sewing supplies, storing gift-wrap gear is an easy leap.

There's a dressmaker's mannequin in one corner. Seth says his mom doesn't use it anymore. I wanted to make our costumes on it, but he says it's only for specially tailored clothing. He says our costume design is much simpler than that.

When they were little, he and Jill spent lots of time in here, Seth says. Lucky for the rest of us in the act, because Sandra, Willow and I know squat about sewing.

Not that everybody in Fashion Show bothers sewing costumes. Some acts wear regular clothes or get props from the dollar store. Last year there was an act that dressed up in baggy animal costumes, which must have been rentals. If you have baggy costumes or big skirts, I've noticed, it helps make the dancing look more pro. The movement and swirl distract from the different ways people move their bodies, as well as any mistakes in steps or timing. That's why we're doing our costumes with a very loose and easy fit. Our tunics will swirl and glitter along with our dance moves.

We've been up here most of the afternoon, and I'm pretty impressed with Seth's knowledge. We drew up basic patterns on craft paper from his mom's rolls of gift wrap. We cut three short dresses, for me, Willow and Sandra. At first Seth would have nothing to do with the shimmer fabric for himself, but I suggested he could make a necktie with the extra, and he got into that idea.

Now he's running seams on his mom's sewing machine. "It's semiprofessional," he tells me, winding thread through tiny hooks and holes. "Double the speed of a regular household sewing machine."

We're working on my tunic first, since I'm here to model it. Seth is already wearing his shiny tie. It hangs loose around an open collar. His shirtsleeves are all rumpled around his elbows. This is the only swag way to wear a tie, Seth insists. He does look cute. He gets this intense frown every time he runs another seam, like he's driving a car or something.

He bites off the thread and slips the tunic over my T-shirt and jeans. In the show, we'll wear these over dark leggings, so the color will really stand out. I swish the fabric, swaying a little, and the dress looks like molten gold. I do some of my moves in front of the mirror.

"Hold on." Seth is coming for me with a pincushion. It's true—the tunic is sliding off one shoulder when I dip forward.

"It still has to be sexy, right?" I remind him. It'd be nice if the costume stayed put, but I'm afraid we're going to lose the fluid lines if he messes with it too much.

"Stop worrying," he growls through a mouthful of pins. "And stop fidgeting."

He releases me, and I do my dip again. This time the tunic stays on. I do a full turn. I move closer to the mirror, trying to figure out what he's done to the neckline. It doesn't look ruined or anything.

"Don't prick yourself," he says. "Take it off, and we'll sew it down."

But I don't want to. I do a half turn, looking over my shoulder at the way the fabric flows down. Seth said something about cutting on the bias. That's why the fabric falls in such a twisty, flowing way. It uses up more fabric, though, which is why the tunic barely covers my butt. As I sway back and forth, I see that it's definitely worth it. The costume accentuates every move, glinting and glittering even in daylight. Imagine it under stage lights.

I smile at my image. "Seth, you're amazing! You've got skills, man." I can see him behind me, leaning against the sewing-machine table. He's got a strange expression on his face, somewhere between surprise and pain. He uncrosses his arms and comes up to the mirror. I can't see his face anymore, but his hands are moving across my shoulders, checking the neckline.

"You look, ah..." Seth's voice has gone scratchy. He clears his throat. "Really, really good."

Everything goes still. I hold my breath. Seth sounds very serious, and we're not usually serious together. I'm so glad I can't see his face right now. Can he see mine in the mirror? I lower my eyes, avoiding my reflection.

"Thank you." It comes out like a squeak. I manage to stutter, "You look really good too." After all, it's what I've been thinking all day. I can at least return a compliment.

I want to turn around—I've been standing in front of this mirror forever—but I'm scared of what will happen if I do. Will he move away? Will he try to kiss me? I don't know which idea scares me more.

"That's the costume?" I jump—practically out of my skin. Seriously, Jill's voice could shatter glass.

Seth scrambles back to the table. I carefully remove the tunic, avoiding pins.

"It looks nice." Jill leans against the doorframe.

"What do you want, JJ?" Seth has buried himself behind the sewing machine. I pass the tunic over. He starts flicking levers, twisting knobs. Jill grabs both sides of the doorway and leans in, giving her shoulders a good stretch. She doesn't actually come in, but she doesn't seem eager to leave either.

"No, I'm just saying. It's a good idea, your costume." She slides down to the floor and plants her feet on the other doorjamb, making herself into a V. I think she's planning to be friendly. I sit on the edge of the armchair, which is already full with Willow's and Sandra's cut-out dresses. Seth's head is down, over the humming machine.

"Our costumes kind of suck." Jill sighs.

I nod, trying for a sympathetic look. I don't know what to say. Jill seems gloomy—distinctly unDonnaesque. I pick up the flat fabric pieces, still pinned to their patterns, and smooth them across my lap. "I chose the material. Seth is the design genius."

Jill laughs. "You can thank Mom for that. Come the apocalypse, Seth and I will be able to make fabulous clothes out of squirrel hide."

A giggle pops out of me. Who knew Jill was so dark?

Then she turns serious. "You'd think Dawn and Sofia would listen to me about our costumes." She goes on to complain about these pale-gray unitards that Sofia's mom picked up at a dance sale. Sofia and Dawn want to add raggedy bandages around the arms and legs to complete the monster look. "But that's the Mummy," Jill is saying. "Frankenstein wore a blazer."

"Frankenstein's outfit is not sexy," Seth says and gestures for me to pass him another tunic. I take my finished dress from him with both hands and lay it across the back of the armchair.

"That's the problem," Jill agrees. She explains that now Dawn and Sofia are obsessing about getting skinny for the unitards instead of polishing their moves for the act. "I left them at Dawn's place, probably *still* clicking on weight-loss ads. They've begun a dieting competition to motivate each other. How stupid is that? They made me promise not to blab to our moms about it."

"It can be hard keeping everyone focused," I say, thinking of Willow storming out mid-rehearsal in the big gym and my little spat with Sandra.

Seth and I were talking about it. We agreed that we should all stay professional and not let our personal stuff get in the way.

"Be cool—eyes on the prize," is how he puts it. He promised to talk to Sandra and Willow if I would forget about what Sandra did to me in singing class.

"Sure, it's our last year doing Fashion Show, but Sofia and Dawn are taking things too far, you know?" Jill's long legs flutter to the ground, and she stands up. Seth hands me another dress, and I pass him the last fabric pieces. Jill shakes out her legs as if they've gone to sleep. She's being super nice about our costumes. "The idea is way smart. It works with every body type and gives good drama."

But when she turns to go, she pauses, a superior expression creeping across her face. She leans into the room again—this time with menace. "If you ever tell what I said about the diet, or your costumes, I'll kill you both." She whips around and stalks off.

Did she really just say that? Prima Donna stings are different from ordinary wounds—they hurt, but you can't say exactly where. I turn to Seth, my mouth hanging wide. Seth rolls his eyes.

Eleven

o you ever think that maybe dreams can tell the future? Last night I dreamed we were in art class, working on our self-portraits.

In real life, the art teacher is making us do self-portraits in a tiny-square collage technique. She's got this massive pile of magazines for us to cut up—old copies of *Canadian Geographic*, *Elle*, *Maclean's*. They're already half shredded from other classes, but they've still got lots of colors and patterns. We're supposed to use little paper squares to build a bigger image of ourselves. And we can work from a mirror if we want, but not a photo. Willow's doing a pretty good likeness of herself with squares from this spread she found on southern Arizona. Sandra's going for a pop art interpretation, à la soup can, or Marilyn Monroe, using lots of intense colors.

I'm going for what our teacher says is a symbolic approach, because I'm adding all this stuff that's important to me. Also, I'm making myself blue—like Krishna in Mom's books on Indian art—just to be different. And I gave myself extra arms to hold my violin, a heart (to represent my friends and family) and a cloud (which is supposed to represent the airy spirit of imagination). I have to admit, I'm regretting all these extra bits. It's getting complicated with the tiny squares. I should have stopped at blue. But if I change now, I'm afraid the teacher will decide I'm not dedicating myself to the project, and give me a lower grade.

Anyway, that's what's really going on in art class. But in my dream last night, it got weird.

In my dream, we were all working at the long, paint-splattered tables. Everyone had their little piles of snipped squares. A couple of kids were over by the magazine stacks, riffling through them. The sun was streaming through the windows. I saw Sandra's hands—complete with green-painted fingernails—brush paste on a square before patting it onto her picture. Willow was standing back to squint at her own work, hair dancing with static in the dry air. She was standing in that way she does, knees bent, shoulders rounded, trying to hide her height.

Then she started whispering to Sandra, who was still gazing down. But I could tell Sandra was listening.

I always work across the table from them—but in this dream it was like they didn't see me. Then something happened to my eyes, or my imagination, and the whole scene broke down into little squares. Except they were more like cubes, because this was a 3-D image.

All the shades and shapes that made up my friends, the bright windows behind them, and the teacher moving through the class, nodding and pointing, were made of these little cubes, or boxes. It was almost like when you blow up the pixels in a computer image, only more real.

And then the cubes that were Sandra shimmered and shifted as she turned to Willow, who was still speaking. (It was like a silent movie, this dream.)

Then Sandra started shaking with laughter, as if Willow had said something funny, and Willow smirked back. She looked up over Sandra's head, straight at me. Willow knew that I was watching. They were laughing about me.

That's when I woke up, my heart thudding. I took a few breaths and rolled over. In the dark, I forced myself to imagine a different scene.

This time Sandra was still looking down at her art, but instead of laughing, she was nodding at what Willow was saying. Willow glanced up, her face brightened, and she waved to me like, *Hey, where did you go? We've been waiting for you!*

That was better. I could breathe again.

In this second version everything looked normal. All the funny cubes were gone. Which makes me think of how many different ways you can look at a thing. Are Willow and Sandra as I usually see them, as solid people? Or are they a collection of possibilities, always shifting and changing? Maybe that's what art is for—to help people make sense of crazy questions.

I don't usually wig out like this, but I've been waiting a long time to try out for Fashion Show.

I want us to at least audition—at least give it our best shot. And I can't do it without Sandra and Willow.

I shake my head to chase away these fluttery thoughts. Dumb dream. So useless.

Twelve

"The curb's coming up," I tell Sandra, who's holding on to the crook of my arm. She's wearing the in-flight sleep mask our drama teacher handed out. All the assigned "blind" people get one. As Sandra's assigned helper, I'm supposed to guide her through the streets. Back in class, we'll all share our experiences. This is what our teacher calls partner work.

We're getting funny looks. But in this neighborhood, people should be used to this kind of thing. Last week the engineering students at the university paraded in pink hard hats, shouting their heads off.

"Ow—crud!" Sandra stumbles up the curb. We've just started, but already she is puffing like an angry dragon. Well, okay, the puffs billowing from her mouth are on account of the cold air. I must look dragon-like too. She peeks from under the sleep mask to see the ground.

"Put it back." I sound like I'm talking to my kindergarten reading partner.

Sandra huffs. "This is stupid. Nobody's here to make us do this, Adina. How about dropping the turbo mode? I vote we blow this off."

I sigh. At least I got her halfway up the hill. "How about we switch? I'll wear the blindfold." We have to keep moving anyway, because it's freezing out here. We may as well do the drama exercise.

Sandra joyfully rips off the flight mask and shoves it on my head. Everything goes dark. Suddenly I notice the sounds and smells of traffic chugging by. I feel someone squeezing past us on the narrow sidewalk.

"Okay, I'll lead—but we're getting fries!" she says.

Fries are a good idea. Our teacher never said we couldn't snack. Sandra grabs my arm and starts pulling me downhill and around the corner. She must be headed for the souvlaki place. They serve a massive cone of fries for only two dollars.

"Watch out!" I'm screaming at the same time as I'm laughing. Her mad dash is making me trip all over myself.

"C'mon, just take the stupid thing off—I'm cold and hungry!" She jerks at my hand and my feet tumble forward. They catch on something, and I go down.

It's as if volts of electricity are shooting through my wrists and knees. For a second I'm on all fours, then I tip over, like a tree. "Ooh..."

People are around me, murmuring, helping me up. I flex one wrist, then the other. Feeling like I'm stuck in slow motion, I push the sleep mask onto my forehead. Then I'm really blinded, the sun is so bright.

"It's partner work," I hear Sandra explaining.

"I'm all right," I assure everyone, blinking as they come into focus. I rub my knees. Sandra holds the door open as I limp into the restaurant. She helps me find a place at a table near the cash register, then gets in the queue to order fries. I pull up my jeans to examine my bruised kneecaps.

"You okay?" Sandra calls. The line creeps forward. She moves forward with it. Now that she's in speaking range, she says, "You should've ditched the mask when I said."

What? The freaking mask is still on my head, so I tear it off and whip it at her.

Sandra picks it up from the floor as she advances a few steps more. "Seriously, Adina. You're way obsessed with doing everything right. It's too much."

I shake my head. *What's she talking about? And by the way, thanks for the apology for smashing up my knees. They'll be fine eventually.*

"I mean, it's not just this. It's everything. Fashion Show."

I sit up. *Where's she going with this?*

"I mean, Dawn trashes your two best friends, and you don't even care. All you think about is your precious show."

That's not quite true. As the line moves forward, Sandra rummages through her jacket for cash. All of a sudden she looks like she might cry.

"We could've reported it," I say. "You didn't want to." I'm not trying to argue, but that's what happened.

"Who cares about reporting? *You* didn't care! What kind of friend doesn't show sympathy?

I know I'm fat"—Sandra's face goes red—"but I have feelings."

I don't know what to say. I guess I *was* thinking about our act. But I put up with stuff from Sandra too. I've got the throbbing patellas to prove it. And there was my humiliation in singing class, don't forget (although, trust me, *I've* been trying to).

"Willow was mad for me. But not you—you're too busy wanting to be perfect!"

I can feel my mouth hanging open. I stop rubbing my knees. Too much is whirling through my head. Sandra and I have always been different. Together we balance. We make a good team. But these days we just get on each other's nerves. Is this what people mean when they talk about friends growing apart? Am I turning into a priss? Is Sandra becoming a mean brute?

I close my mouth. The greasy air in here is making me feel sick. *Can't we all just get along? At least until Fashion Show?* I remember Seth's advice when we were making costumes. *Be cool,* he said. *Eyes on the prize.*

Sandra looks at me as if she can hear everything in my head. She jams the flight mask into her pocket, steps out of line and stomps out the door.

"Sandra, wait—"

Just. Freaking. Perfect. I take a deep breath, push myself up and hobble back to drama class.

* * *

I arrive late. Another partner team is bragging how they made twelve dollars in change by sitting on the corner, holding out a cap.

"So why do you call this theater and not begging?" the teacher asks while giving me the hairy eyeball. Willow tucks up her legs so I can lean back against the armchair she's sitting in. We hold drama class in the so-called lounge off the cafeteria. Kids are sitting everywhere—on the arms of sofas, on the side tables and on the floor, like me.

"Oh, that's easy, man. I was singing. I had my eyes closed," one partner explains.

The other joins in. "Yeah, he was doing a Stevie Wonder head sway and everything, ha-ha!"

They both break down in laughter, fending off a flurry of high fives and fist bumps from their neighbors.

"All right, all right," the teacher says, looking around the room. "Anyone else?" His gaze rests on me. He's picking on me because I got back late. I consider showing the injuries sustained in our little drama, but Sandra jumps in.

"Adina and I both took a turn being blind." She's staring hard at me, like I'm going to say something different. "I think we both see a little better now." She makes it sound like a threat.

But the teacher likes her answer. He thinks it's profound.

"Look, I'm sorry." I finally catch up with Sandra by our lockers. "You're right, okay? I should have stood up for you—or stood by you—before with Dawn. I didn't realize she hurt your feelings. But I should've, because what she said was messed up."

Sandra looks into my eyes for a while. She's trying to figure out if I mean it. Well, I do, because it's true. And someone has to apologize first, right?

Thirteen

We're all in Seth's rec room, resplendent in our costumes. Sandra and Willow love them as much as I do. How could they not? We're fabulous in them!

They're twirling and twisting to see if the fit is all right. Their necklines slip like mine did, so Seth starts upstairs for a needle and thread.

"Can you do that later?" I plead. He knows I don't have long to practice. My brother has a hockey game, and my parents are forcing me to go with them.

I turn on Seth's mix and we do a quick run-through. We're not too bad.

"Willow, you lag on your way back to the line," I tell her. "It's got to be *bam, bam, bam.*" I snap my fingers at each beat. "Let's try that bit again."

I cue the music and hurry into place. "There, like that." *Snap, snap, snap.* "Better—good!" Willow could lighten up on the scowling, but I don't say anything because at least her time is tighter. Besides, the costumes are making our moves really swing. "Let's keep going—looks good, Sandra!"

As Sandra sashays by, she flashes me a massive eye roll. "Take it easy, Cheer Squad."

But I've got bigger problems than Sandra being snotty, because Seth is flubbing his helicopter move. This happens about half the time, which makes me nervous.

So long as he's swinging his leg forward, it slides under each arm and the other leg, fast and smooth, over and over. But he insists on changing direction too. When he tries spinning his leg in a backward circle, it catches. It's weak.

"Seth, forget it. Just do it forward. It will look worse if you mess up."

"Then how 'bout you shut up, so I can get it right?" he says through gritted teeth.

No problem. We'll keep two-stepping forever, while you struggle on. Fine. I won't mention it again.

But if I *were* to say something more, I'd tell him the problem is not only the helicopter move itself. What I'd tell him—even though he snapped at me—is how frustrated he gets when he flubs his helicopter, and how it ruins his concentration for the rest of the act. In front of the judges, we can't afford to have Seth dancing as if he'd rather be anywhere else.

"We need more water," I say instead.

Rushing upstairs to the kitchen, I remind myself we have a great act. I go through it in my head, step by step. I see us moving down the runway, the judges watching from the side. Sandra, Seth and I are in a row, doing a slide-dip-slide move, as Willow shimmies in front, making her flashlight shine.

I know our act is as good as anything I've seen in all my years watching Fashion Show. Especially when you include the flashlights and costumes. If we can perform it slick and sharp, I *know* the judges will choose us for the show.

But then I see Willow flaking out, doing all her moves backward or something equally Willowesque. I see Sandra hardly trying when she's in backup position—overdoing her ambitious-singer character and messing up the act as a whole. And I see Seth dancing like a sulky zombie because of a helicopter fail. I'm so wrapped up in my thoughts, I'm already at the kitchen sink before I notice the Prima Donnas are here too. I screech.

"Sorry!" My laugh sounds like I'm choking. "I didn't see you guys."

Jill's at the table, her long legs tucked up, crumbling a half-eaten muffin. Sofia's sprawled across from her, most unballerina-like. Dawn's leaning against the counter. As I reach for the tap to refill my water jug, Dawn puts her finger on her lips, like I should be quiet. Ghostly scraps of conversation are coming up through the heating vent.

"...driving me up the wall..."

"...tell her to chill."

"I doubt she's gonna go for that..."

I put my hands against the sink to steady myself. The Donnas are listening to how much my friends hate me right now. I think this is a new low for me.

They're all staring at me. I can feel my face wobble into a weak smile. I pray to dissolve into nothingness before their eyes—at least it would be a spectacular exit. Then I wouldn't have to go back downstairs either.

When that doesn't happen, I refill the water jug instead. I'll go back down and face the music. I'm sure it'll make excellent heating-vent entertainment for the Donnas.

"You're right, you know." Dawn leans over to grab some of Jill's muffin. "They're not taking it seriously. And they need to, if they want to be good."

What did she say? The water's spilling over the jug, but I'm too frozen with shock to move. No one's ever agreed with my turbo ways before—except maybe my parents.

"You think?" My voice is tiny. I switch off the tap and slowly turn around. Maybe they're making fun.

But they're not. They're looking at me like I'm a human being—like we share a common interest. Which I guess we do—the fine art of Fashion Show.

It feels like three beautiful guardian angels have descended. Or like I'm Dorothy, new in Oz, watching the approach of three good witches, floating in glowing bubbles.

"Yeah. Right?" My voice is louder this time. I feel strong again. Buoyant and bouncy. I can do this. I can make the act perfect. I can make Seth, Willow and Sandra see the light.

"You've got some nice ideas going down there," Sofia concedes.

Jill gives me a smirk. "We were spying."

That's okay! That's totally okay! I want to ask them for any notes they might have. In drama, notes are when the director tells you how much you suck. But I can't make any changes to the act now. I've already got my hands full with the gang downstairs. "No, look, spying is great." I really appreciate their interest. "I'm sorry about—all that—at the gym—" I wave my hands and make a crazy face to show how I go a little nuts sometimes.

Dawn nods. "Yeah, I'm kinda sorry too. I shouldn't be making fatty comments, especially when I'm such a tub myself." She stares at the morsel of muffin in her hand and puts in on the counter.

"*You're* a tub? What about me?" Sofia sits up, lifts her shirt and struggles to pull a scrawny pinch of skin off her abs.

Jill turns to me. Her eyes are massively crossed. She looks hilarious—I burst out laughing. Sofia and Dawn look offended.

"Sorry," I splutter. "She just—" I gesture toward Jill. Of course I'm not going to contradict the Donnas, not when they're being nice to me, but they have clearly lost their minds. Then, as I turn toward Dawn, something worse pops out instead.

"Maybe you should apologize to Sandra," I say.

I can't believe I said that out loud.

Dawn narrows her eyes at me. I hold my breath.

"Maybe I will," she says.

I grab the jug and take off before I can open my big mouth again.

* * *

Downstairs, they're waiting for me.

"Adina, we have to talk," Willow says.

Things must be extreme if Willow is speaking for the group. The others probably don't trust themselves to be civil. Well, they should be more mature, because we've got a fine act. We just need to get consistent with our performance.

I remain standing. I hope my example will encourage them to get back to practicing. I try for a friendly yet professional expression. They don't need to know I already heard what they think.

"We think you can stop being bossy now. Nobody made you queen, you know." Sandra takes the water jug to fill our cups.

"That's not what we said," Willow blurts out, glaring at Sandra. "We just think that maybe you're..." She's tugging on her hair like she does when she's giving presentations in class. It means she's searching for words. "We're not dancers, Adina, and you seem to forget that."

"Speak for yourself." Seth leans back into the couch, his hands linked behind his head. "I'm badass at dancing. My moves be smooth."

I've got to smile. His moves be *mostly* smooth. But Seth's done so much for this act, when I think of it. He mixed the music. He did the costumes—basically by himself. He brought in the flashlights, and his break-dancing solo is one of our highlights.

Then my phone alarm goes off. There's no time to argue. I've got to be outside on the front porch in five minutes, waiting for my family to pick me up.

"Okay. I agree." What else can I say? "But let's have one last run-through. Let's make it our best ever."

Fourteen

ow, waiting for everyone at Coffee Hut, I've got butterflies in my stomach. It's like the night before a big test. Or when the dentist is coming at your face with a giant steel needle full of Novocain. It's not a good feeling. Fashion Show auditions are tomorrow.

We're not ready. We're not good enough. I mean—maybe we're okay.

I wish I felt more confident about the act, considering all the stress and strife that's gone into it. I feel like it should be...well, something *more*, you know? *I* should feel more cool, more accomplished. But instead I feel as insignificant as when I was a little kid in the audience, gazing up at the teenagers on the runway.

The only difference is now it's *my* butt on the line. Is this stage fright? Because none of this is how I dreamed it would be.

And it's not helping that all the other Coffee Hut customers are staring as they pass my table. I know I look like a doof. Here I am at a big table, just me and four large iced mocha lattes with extra whipped cream. I look like I have imaginary friends. Or, worse, that these fluffy drinks of sweet deliciousness *are* my friends.

It's not my fault the others are late. I sip the drink in front of me. I'm beginning to wonder if this was such a good idea after all. With my used-up Coffee Hut card, I tap out a beat against the table. Buying a round of special coffees seemed like a great way to get everyone in a team spirit again. I was trying for positivity and good leadership, but right now it feels more like a bribe. A bribe that no one seems to want.

I almost don't recognize myself. For the past while, the way my insides have been feeling and the way I've been acting—it hasn't been matching up. I've been trying to be chill, like Seth says. I've been pretending I think the act is good enough when I know it can be better. How come Sandra gets to vent her usual snarkiness while I'm killing myself to smooth everything over?

Because auditions are tomorrow, that's why. Because my dream is to be in Fashion Show.

"Take a picture, why don't you," I murmur around my straw. These two businessmen are staring at me. They've got Bluetooth phones coming out their ears. They start circling my table, as if they deserve it more than me. One of them is now closing in to say something. *Please, please,* I pray, *let him be interrupted by an important call. I deserve this table as much as anyone.*

"Seth!" I jump up and practically knock whipped cream all over the businessman's suit. "Over here!" I'm waving like a fool, I'm so relieved. How could I think no one would show up? These are my friends. Fashion Show is making me crazy.

Seth puts his bundle on a seat, then comes around to sit next to me. I push a latte toward him. "Is that for Sandra and Willow?" I ask, eyes on the plastic bag. Seth must have finished the alterations on their costumes. Before he can answer, I tell him, "They're late."

"Yup, I see that." He takes a long pull on his straw. The whipped cream lowers in the cup. I go back to sipping my drink, eyes shifting to the door. Why aren't they here by now?

"How many coffees have you been drinking?" Seth looks at me sideways. He scoops whipped cream, using his straw like a lever.

"Just this one. Why?" I can't stop checking the door. It's swinging open and closed, open and closed. People pass in and out, letting in a whoosh of cold air every time. None of them are Sandra and Willow.

Finally, I have a sighting. "Oh, there's Willow!" I pop up again, do my mad wave, and Willow floats our way. I push a latte at her as she takes a seat. "Where's Sandra?" Sandra and Willow are both in the woodwind chamber-music group—I figured they'd be coming together after practice.

Willow shrugs. She's got this dazed, blank expression on her face. Seth hustles her back to standing, pulling out her costume. He takes her drink from her hand, putting it on the table.

"Wasn't Sandra with you at chamber group?" I raise my voice a little, because Willow may not be able to hear me with the costume over her head like that.

"What?" Her voice is muffled by ripples of gold.

I try a little louder. "I said—"

But a look from Seth stops me. He's mouthing something—I have no idea what. But his eyebrows are low, practically crossing in the middle, so maybe I don't want to know. I get the general message.

I slump back in my chair and make straw noises with the melting ice chips in my cup. Seth is tugging on the costume and trying to get Willow to stand straight. Why is everyone being so difficult?

I close my eyes and think of Florida. Not that Florida is my happy place or anything. It's because when our family visited the Everglades, there was this murky, thick, still water. It was full of vines and weeds and general grossness— all tangling around snakes and alligators. At the time, I felt lucky to be skimming the surface of the whole mess in an airboat. Now it feels like I'm waist deep in it, calling everyone from their wanderings in the reeds, trying to shove them toward dry land. Don't you hate it when people don't understand what's good for them?

The whipped cream on Sandra's coffee must be defluffing by now. I could open my eyes to check, but knowing would only make me feel worse. Has she decided to ditch us? No, I firmly tell myself, don't think like that—Sandra wouldn't do that. Sandra knows that if she bails, the act is ruined. The whole number leads up to her grand finale. If we have to audition without it, our act will end in a sad *pffft*. Sandra absolutely has to show.

"Is Adina napping or something?"

My eyes flip open. Sandra's standing before me, hand on hip, slurping coffee. *Relief!*

All my muscles go limp, like I've been holding my breath for the last half hour. Then I jump up, but since there's nothing for me to do, I sit back down. Seth starts in with his costume magic, and Sandra submits as if she was born to be fussed over. Willow is finishing her coffee, gleaming in gold, while catching up Sandra on their music homework. Everyone's finally here.

So why am I annoyed?

"You guys look great!" I'm trying for cheerful, but it sounds fake even to me. All three of them turn and stare. I want to dump coffee dregs over their heads, but that would ruin the costumes. I realize no one's apologized for being late. No one has thanked me for the drinks. I realize I hate my friends.

But I'm stuck with them, at least until Fashion Show is over. I'm not going through all this only to give up at the last minute. I won't go turbo all over them—as they would say—even though they deserve it. There's too much at stake.

Don't you hate having to rely on other people?

Fifteen

There are masses of us back here—all in pre-audition panic. This is nuts.

There's no real backstage in our auditorium. For Fashion Show, a huge curtain divides the stage in half. There's plenty of room left up front, plus there's the runway.

The stage is deep, because it has to hold a large choir and a full-sized orchestra. But even in this big space, we're pushing and shoving. People are running around, trying to find their fellow performers. Costumes are breaking down. Panicked scream-whispers hiss though the crowd. But we have to keep quiet out of respect for the act up front, auditioning before the judges.

"Boyz to Zen! We're ready for you!" A group breaks out of the crowd. I recognize them from the junior a cappella chorus. They're wearing bow ties, and they've spray-painted their hair Day-Glo green. One kid looks like he accidentally sprayed his face too. They disappear behind the curtain. The perky sounds of a scratchy, old version of "April Showers" filters backstage.

"Where's Willow?" I ask. We're up pretty soon.

Seth has planted himself by the curtain. He's gelled his hair into spikes. It looks as if he's slept in his shirt, probably to get the wrinkles just right. His tie glistens as he curses the sound guy—or maybe the sound system. Everything sounds okay to me.

Sandra's laughing at him. "Chill out, goofus. All that gel must be seeping into your brain."

It's not only her tone, like she knows better than everyone else. And it's not only that Seth has been working like a dog to make this happen, and she could have some respect. And it's not her dirty trick in singing class, or that she practically ripped off my kneecaps during drama exercises—although both are flooding back now, almost as if I'm living them again.

It's all of it. The pressure, the details. All the hoops I've been jumping through. Mostly on account of Sandra. Something inside me snaps.

"Shut up, you!" I'm whispering, but I make sure my glare is harsh. "At least Seth cares about the act—he's put in a ton of work. What have you done? Besides prancing around like a miffed diva, that is. You've been grand at that!"

Sandra's eyes widen, and she goes pale. She doesn't snap back, as I might expect. She doesn't nod and get on with it, like I'd hope. Instead she turns and walks away. She's going... She's left. She bumps past Willow, who's arriving late, as usual.

Just. Freaking. Perfect.

If we weren't backstage right now, having to be quiet, I would be screaming my head off. Willow is waving goodbye to Sandra's back— clueless as ever. Could I have chosen two more difficult friends? They're like stones in my shoe. I'd punch a wall to get rid of these shakes in my hands, but there's nothing around except curtain—and soft bodies.

Don't tempt me, I tell myself.

The Day-Glo bow ties come rustling back through the curtain, brushing past us. I can feel the heat coming off them. They are practically buzzing, they're so thrilled with their performance. Congratulations to them. I hope they broke legs all over the place. I hope they have to drag themselves home on bleeding stumps. The next act hustles onstage. It's an all-girl act this time, dressed in hoodies, ballcaps and low baggies. They're already in character, full of limping swagger, as they disappear behind the curtain.

Our costumes are prettier.

When I realize I've backed myself to a wall, I lean against it—and slowly sink to the floor. I don't want to punch anymore or scream. I want to pass out.

Seriously, I'm feeling a bit faint. Willow is talking to me, but I can't hear anything through the mist. She's pulled off her tunic. She's handing it to Seth, waving in the direction that Sandra went. I put my head between my knees, and the blood begins rushing back.

It's all gone boots up. All the work, all the stress, and now my dream is shot. I couldn't make it happen. I couldn't even bring it to audition—which is the true fail, now that I think about it.

"I'm kind of relieved," I hear Willow saying. "It turns out that Fashion Show is not really my thing, you know?"

When I look up, she's gone. Seth is kneeling over me. "Are you okay?" It's the worried expression on his face that does me in. Have you ever noticed how the most horrible things may be happening to you, but it's easy to keep it together—until someone shows a bit of sympathy, and you turn into a blubbing mess? I bury my face in his shoulder so no one can see me cry.

Sixteen

I t's up to Seth and me to tell the judges our act is wrecked, and we won't be auditioning. We keep to the shadowy edges of the stage as we creep around the curtain. It's not difficult to hide. The stage lights are bright on the runway, and there's plenty of distraction from the swagger-girls running back, holding up their jeans and punching the air.

By the time we get behind the judges' table, the next act is coming on. Wouldn't you know, it's the Prima Donnas.

Sometimes life comes along and kicks you in the stomach. Then sometimes, as you're going down, it smashes your nose into your head. It's bad enough seeing another act audition. That it turns out to be the fabulous Donnas is making my eyes tear up again. Now I get to watch how it's really done—the opposite of failure. My nose pricks. I sniffle.

They're wearing the dreaded unitards. Jill's put on a tattered denim miniskirt too. They've teased and piled their hair à la Bride of Frankenstein. They're clomping into position in towering platform shoes. I'm impressed they plan to dance in those. Plus, their monster-goth eye makeup is very effective.

The music goes on. I recognize the hard horn riff at the front even before the drums come in. They've chosen "X Gon' Give It To Ya" (must be the clean version). The Donnas start their act lying down. I get it—they're being Frankenstein before he comes to life. As the vocals come in, growling low, they start twitching.

And then, as DMX is saying, *"Listen up, listen—hear it, hear it,"* the Donnas go all stiff, like they've been shot full of electricity. Then they sit up fast—*whoosh!*—arms outstretched.

I can't help feeling shivers as they each do their own version of a stiff-limbed monster struggling to its feet. The platform shoes convey an amazing, clunky vibe. As always, Sofia's dance training shows in her clean, expressive moves.

They're moving in sync now, stomping forward, off in three directions, then back together. They bump into one another, turning into a dancing monster knot. Jill's got great rhythm, and Dawn knows how to be funny.

Excellent moves, amazing music, cool theme. I can feel the thrill start down in my stomach, just like at last year's Fashion Show, and the year before. The Prima Donnas are killing it. And I'm sad and glad and grateful I get to watch.

They're popping and locking their way forward, platform shoes sliding under stiff knees. They move into triangular formation to squat into some light twerking before they stomp off in three directions, stiff arms and legs flailing.

From back here, I see the judges fidget and murmur at the twerking, but the sexy moves are gone before anyone can get too upset. Plus, the ugly Franken-moves are pure genius for taking the edge off twerking in a unitard. In the shadows, I'm smiling and swaying, and I can feel Seth grooving next to me. DMX is singing, "*Ka-blam—open that door, for real!*"

You've got to hand it to those Donnas.

Halfway down the runway they start doing partner stuff. Jill falls back, one platform foot outstretched. Dawn catches her and pushes her upright again. Then Dawn swoons and falls toward Sofia's arms. That heavy shoe must take some strength to lift high, but she looks good—very Frankenstein. Only this time, something happens with Sofia, who isn't ready to catch her.

Sofia looks like she's dizzy. Her hands go for her head instead of Dawn's shoulders, and she totters—not a good idea in those platforms. She cries out as Dawn crashes into her and they both go down...and over.

I can't believe it—they've fallen off the runway! Jill shrieks. The music stops. The judges rush out from behind their table. The tallest (our bass choir singing teacher) vaults off the runway to where Sofia is wailing below. The other two judges (our English and drama teachers) take the stairs. They huddle over the girls, asking them to move their arms and legs.

"I told you guys!" Jill is yelling down at them like a crazy person. "You have to eat!" She stamps in her dangerous shoes. "Now look what you've done!"

Below, Sofia tries to stand. She cries out, collapsing against our singing teacher. The English teacher is shaking her head and clucking, "Stay off the ankle, darling." Sofia begins to sob. The singing teacher carries her from the auditorium. I can't imagine her tears are just from the hurt ankle. Sofia is used to being in pain from her intense ballet training.

"Is she all right?" Jill's tear-stained face turns in confusion, and Seth and I rush over. "I told them they were being stupid—they weren't eating!" The other two teachers are still patting down Dawn for injuries while she unlaces her shoes to stand up. Dawn seems okay.

Kids from backstage start trickling in, then flooding, to see what's going on. Our drama teacher rushes up the stage steps, waving everyone back. She bellows in her powerful actor voice, "Everyone go home! All acts that haven't auditioned, we'll hold an extra session after school on Friday!"

Seventeen

"**F**riday!" Seth and I look at each other and groan. He must be thinking the same thing as me. We still have an audition slot, but no act. How ironic is that? On the stage floor, Jill is kicking off her platforms, muttering about the nurse's office and finding her friends.

"They better be okay," she growls, "or I'll kill them."

Seth pulls her off the floor. He ties the laces of her shoes together while she smears teary makeup across her face. I don't have a tissue on me, so I offer the sleeve of my shirt. It's pretty clean.

"Go ahead," I insist. "Your sleeve is so pale, you'll muck it up completely." We must look odd as we leave the auditorium together, Jill dabbing her eyes with my arm, Seth with a pair of honking-big platform shoes hanging around his neck.

I'll bet Sofia and Dawn are wishing they hadn't got so carried away dieting for their act. I can't believe I'm thinking it, but maybe they took Fashion Show a little too far.

* * *

Well, this is disturbing. Sofia is super upset. She has to go to Emergency. Her mother is here and everything.

Sofia's ankle looks like a balloon, and every time she tries to stand on it, she starts crying again. Her mom keeps begging her to stop, but Sofia wants so badly for the ankle to be okay.

It doesn't look okay.

"I'll be fine! We'll just go home and ice it— Mommy, please?" Sofia sounds like a little kid. The school nurse and her mom keep shaking their heads. Even I can see that Sofia is kidding herself.

"A doctor will look at your ankle, sweetheart." Sofia's mom has that overly calm voice, the one parents get when they are *freaking* on the inside.

"That ankle needs an X-ray." The school nurse is offering pills and a paper cup of water. "For the emergency-room wait," she suggests to Sofia's mom, showing her the bottle. Sofia's mom nods.

Dawn and Jill are huddled around Sofia. They don't look like the Prima Donnas anymore. They look like wounded sparrows. Since we got here, Sofia's ankle has been changing color, going a scary blue-purple as yellowing skin stretches around the swelling. I'm trying not to run to the bathroom and hide. Why doesn't anyone take charge and get her out of here? She needs a hospital now!

The thing is, even Seth and I know why everyone is being so patient and careful, and why Sofia is trying to pretend her ankle is all right. It has nothing to do with missing out on the stupid fashion show. Sofia is really serious about ballet. She does a class every day—more on weekends. I heard that she was accepted into a ballet school out west this year but decided to finish high school here first. So if Sofia's ankle is messed up, what does that do to her dance career?

"I can't believe this is happening!" Sofia lets out a fresh wail, while Jill and Dawn murmur and twitter, stroking her shoulders, smoothing her hair.

On the nurse's desk, the phone rings. "The taxi is out front, Sofia. It's time to go."

We all troop to the front hall, Sofia propped between Jill and Dawn. Her mom's lugging all her school junk, plus the boot Sofia can't get on her foot. Good thing it isn't snowing yet.

Standing in the great front hall, watching Sofia struggle down the school steps, across the yard and into the cab, I suddenly feel really tired. Only a short while ago I was backstage, weeping all over Seth. I feel kind of embarrassed now. There are worse things than missing an audition, right? I just want to go to my locker, get my stuff and go home. It's been a long day.

I turn around to see Seth, Jill and Dawn by the benches, heads together. It looks like an intense conversation. Above them, the masks of smiling Comedy and frowning Tragedy are carved into the wall. A swirly carved ribbon connects them, showing how they are two sides of a greater whole. After years of drama class, I can figure that out.

Pale marble floors lead to the red-carpeted inner hallway, which is also the vestibule of the auditorium. Right now an exhibition of sculptures by the eleventh-graders is installed in there.

But come concert time, that's where masses of kids in their concert uniforms will queue with their instruments. Inside the auditorium, hundreds of seats will be filled with relatives waiting to hear them play. It's pretty cute when the little ones have a concert. They're made to sit on the floor in tidy groups—like rows of baby soldiers, or stubby lawn gnomes—while their teachers patrol the edges.

I can hear Seth and the others talking about Sofia, and something about the act. What act? Jill and Dawn have lost their star performer. Their toss-and-turn moves require three dancers. And, of course, Seth and I have no act anymore.

I wander over to the massive bronze plaque that covers the wall next to the reception kiosk. The receptionist has long gone home. I should too—as soon as I get the energy to climb four flights up to my locker.

In all my time at the school, I never really looked at this plaque. It's a kind of monument. I have to look way up to read the heading, which says, *Former pupils and masters who served in the Great War 1914–18*. In history class we call it World War I. I guess when they made this wall, they didn't know there'd be another world war coming along shortly.

This thought does nothing to cheer me up. It's strange to think of students like us going to war. I bet they didn't stress about Fashion Show.

"Adina, what do you think?" Seth calls over. Then he turns back to Jill and Dawn. "We could combine the best moves from each act—make it like a battle between backup singers and monster dancers."

"Except this time, Dawn and I will wear combat boots." Jill has a grim, no-fooling look on her face. Dawn gazes on their platform shoes, heaped on the bench. She nods reluctantly.

I get what they're thinking. Our disco-glimmer and their Franken-goth, together in one act. If anyone can make it work, it's the Donnas and Seth. But in time for auditions on Friday?

"I'll catch up with you guys tomorrow." My voice echoes across the empty hall. Everything can wait until tomorrow.

"Okay, but hold up a sec." Seth's got his hand raised like he's stopping traffic. "What about Sandra? Do we ask her to join?"

"*Gawd*, Sandra." I feel my shoulders slump. My head drops forward until I'm staring at my scuffed sneakers. They go in and out of focus until I shut my eyes. "Can we think about that tomorrow?"

Eighteen

inally, home at last. I'm stretched out on our massive sectional sofa that Mom currently has set up in an L shape around the family TV. We've got a satellite console, Dev's old Xbox—we've even still got that motion-detector add-on, stuck to the top of the TV. It's been years since we played any of those games—*River Raft, Dance Mania.* I suddenly realize that these days none of us use our home entertainment system. Now we watch our stuff all over the house, from whatever pad, pod or cell phone we're holding at the moment. For old times' sake, I click the Xbox into life.

I should be doing violin practice, but I'm too limp to get up. I am completely wrung out. I scroll through the Xbox options. *The Wolf*

Among Us is in the game-disc tray. Yuck. I press *Play* anyway. The intro movie starts. It's a close-up of a dented trash can. It rattles, and the lid slides off with a clang as a scruffy cat springs out and dashes offscreen.

This is the first time in ages that my brain hasn't been busy with Fashion Show. It should be a relief. It *is* a relief. But it also feels empty, if that makes any sense. The act was taking over my life, and now it's not there anymore.

I wanted everything to be perfect, but it seemed like I'd solve one problem and two more would pop up. It reminds me of when I volunteered at the Y day camp this past summer. I had to put away the kids' floaty toys so the old ladies could use the pool for their aquafit class.

Walking around in the shallow end, I was using one of those noodle floats like a sweeper. I had the idea I was going to sweep all the toys into the stair area and then gather them up. But every time a toy escaped my noodle, I'd make a new wave trying to get it back in line, causing more toys to bob away. Which is pretty much how I was feeling about our act for Fashion Show by the end.

At least with the floaty toys, it took me about five seconds to realize I'd be better off grabbing each one and hurling it poolside. If only Fashion Show could have been solved so easily. Instead, I got more and more wound up, and then—*poof*—it was all taken from me. Everything I'd been working for was gone like a puff of smoke. All my dreaming and my planning—it was like they didn't count for anything. I never imagined that could happen. I guess I always figured if I wanted something enough, and worked hard for it, everything would go as I hoped.

Onscreen, the video is panning across a run-down city neighborhood—smashed cars, boarded-up windows. A homeless lady sits on a doorstep, drinking from a bottle in a crumpled paper bag. The cat runs by.

Take Sofia's ankle, for example. I mean, she's got real problems, right? No fashion-show act is worth that.

Oh, here we go—the story is going to make me choose what happens next. Dev likes this game. The idea is that all these fairy-tale characters are stuck in our world, and they have to hide. I'm sure the homeless lady and the cat will turn out to be fairy-tale creatures. Right now, there's a redheaded kid named Fox trying to jack one of the old cars while a massive guy in a tank top is threatening him with a tire iron. This big guy is going to be a giant in disguise, or an ogre. But I have only a few seconds to choose from the options for what happens next or the story will continue in default mode.

"Guess what?" I tell the screen. "I don't care!"

So the guy with the tire iron chases Fox away and goes back inside.

"If you let the story run on its own, it's going to be very boring." Dev has come out of his room—he must have heard the game. I make space for him on the couch. He picks up the controller and starts clicking, popping up a new screen and adjusting all kinds of settings. "I thought you hated this game."

"I'm not really playing. I'm bumming about the fashion show." I stretch my arms and feel my neck crackle. At least Dev has got me sitting up again. As he clicks forward through the game at lightning speed, I tell him all the sad details of my life. He's obviously not interested, but it makes me feel better.

"Fashion Show always causes drama," he says as Fox sprints through dark hallways with a little toad leaping after him. Dev starts clicking madly. Fox and the toad are in a fistfight. "Last year we had trouble borrowing a trumpet. Dawn was in tears when she thought I was going to have to use my French horn." Dev is sniggering, but I don't know if it's because of the French horn or because Fox flattened the toad.

"I can see Dawn's point of view," I admit. "No offense, but French horn is not as cool as trumpet."

"I don't know." Dev sighs as he puts the game on hold. He leans back so his head rests along the low, puffy top of the sofa. He stares at the ceiling. "I always thought it would be easier the older I got, but problems have a way of growing up with you, you know?"

Uh, no. I *don't* know. Everything's easier for Dev now that he's expected to graduate this spring. Mom and Dad never pester him about homework assignments. I don't think he even has a curfew anymore.

But I don't say it out loud, because Dev never talks to me like this. So I burrow deeper into my corner of the sofa and hug my knees up to my chest. I nod as if I totally relate.

"I'm sick of this school thing year after year—it's enough. If I want to take a year off and travel in India, what's the harm, right?" He slides his head around to look at me for a second, then rolls it back to the ceiling.

What? What's Dev talking about? He's doing pre-engineering next year.

Dev glances at me out of the corner of his eye. "Didn't you know? You must have heard me talking with Mom and Dad about it." He closes his eyes. "You must have heard Dad yelling."

I never heard anything. "What do you want to do in India?" I ask, which may seem a stupid question, because we have tons of family in India, and there are our roots to explore and all that. But Dev has never been into that kind of thing. "Oh, wait—your music?"

Dev's eyes widen like he's thinking, *Way to figure it out, Sherlock.* "They've sent me to a music school since I was four years old—what do they expect?"

He's got a point. Mom and Dad expect us to excel in music, but only as a hobby to make us well-rounded. They must be freaking to think of Dev trying to make it something more.

"I told Dad I'd come back after a year and do the degree. *Just give me a break, okay?* They should be happy I'm interested. They're always babbling about moving back to India. Auntie Lakshmi would put me up—and cousin Govind. I would still be working and learning—about music, that's all."

I see Dev with a dusty backpack, hopping crowded trains for different cities and towns. I see him in market squares, listening to street musicians. I see him playing tabla and dhol. I see him at raves, checking out new DJs, and in traditional nightclubs where musicians sit on the floor and play ragas for hours on end. And I can see why our parents don't want him to go. But what Dev wants to do is really cool.

"Dev, I hope you get your wish!"

Dev's frown softens and his eyes crinkle, like he's about to smile. He's looking down at my hands. They're clasped, just like we used to do when we were little and we really wanted something. We used to kneel under this painting Mom has—a traditional-style picture of a wedding couple. We must have thought they were gods, because we'd clasp our hands and ask for kids' stuff, like McDonald's for dinner or a snow day from school. Dev must be remembering the same thing, because he clasps his hands too.

* * *

We're in Dev's room listening to some tracks. "When Pandas Attack," he calls it. I don't know if that's the band or the name of the tune. I let the sweet melody drift over me, supported by the gentle *tap-tap* of the percussion. The sounds of old-style-recording crackle, water dripping and some kind of animal squawk weave around one another. It's like being taken to another world.

While Dev is playing me his sound tour of Indian electronica, I've been telling him the whole story of Fashion Show, what happened to us and to the Donnas.

"Whoa—poor Sofia." He reaches into the bar fridge under his desk and hands me a Coke. "All she talks about is ballet school in Alberta."

I'm careful when I pop the can so it doesn't spill. We're on the rug, shoulders propped against

the futon mattress he chose to replace his old bed.
Mom was disgusted that Dev wanted to sleep on
the floor, but he got his way in the end. Outside
his window, the trees are bare. I tell him about
the new act that Seth, Jill and Dawn are planning
and how I almost feel like it's too much trouble.

"I never thought I'd give up on Fashion
Show—I've been wanting this forever."

"You're just burned out," Dev assures me.
"If the others are still into it, let them take over
for a while."

That's a thought. I consider it as the music
fades. Yeah—what if I just let go? What would
happen then? Dev clicks on another track. In this
one, whisper vocals come in under an eerie riff of
keyboards.

What about Sandra? Seth's voice comes back
to me as if it's still echoing through the front hall
at school. *Do we ask her to join?*

Whenever I think about Sandra, that's when
I most want to quit Fashion Show. I haven't told
Dev anything about Sandra and me. I don't know
why. I haven't really sorted it out for myself,
I guess. I'm not ready to talk about it like it's a story.

So what is it?

It's as if all the wild, wacky things I love about Sandra are blowing up out of control, like tumors. Talk about turbo.

But maybe, if I'm being honest, some of my own tumors have been getting pretty big too. She's right that I like things to be perfect. I probably get hard-core about it.

That day in the big gym, I could've dropped everything and sympathized with Sandra, I know she's sensitive about her weight. What's the loss of one practice, right? Especially when you consider how the act ended up anyway. Sometimes plans don't turn out the way you expect.

But Sandra went too far. She could've apologized for the singing trick. She shouldn't have knocked me over when I was blindfolded. She could've accepted my apology instead of holding a grudge.

So what is it? I ask myself—and finally stop avoiding the answer. I feel like Sandra hasn't been acting like a friend.

No wonder I'm tired. I gulp down my Coke. I guess I let Sandra down. But she let me down too. So the question is, will our friendship get through it?

The track is filling with more synth layers, and my head starts moving to the beat. Dev is doing the same. He's staring out the window, but I can tell his eyes are really on the music.

"If you need another guy for the act, I can do it," he says.

It's funny what happens when you let go. At the beginning of this year, I never would have dreamed the Donnas would be in our act. And now here's Dev offering too! We're still bobbing our heads in unison, nodding. *Yes, yes, yes.*

"Hey, thanks, Dev." The tune trails out as the next begins. "But you've got enough on your plate. We'll be okay." *Yes, yes, yes.*

Nineteen

The bus is pulling away from the metro station. I'm in the best spot, at the front of the raised level. I like to sit high, but if I go too far back, I get motion sickness. My iPod is playing my new fave download, DJ Megan Hamilton doing a set at some club last week. I bet Seth'll like it too.

I'm going to his place. We're all meeting for a massive-blast rehearsal of the combined disco-monster act. The audition is tomorrow.

Whoa! The bus lurches to a sudden stop, and I almost fall into the stroller in the aisle. The bus driver opens the door and a passenger rushes on, huffing and puffing. It's Sandra.

Yeah, we invited her to join the new act. Not that I made the decision. I was taking Dev's advice about letting go.

As Sandra moves down the aisle, she sees me perched in my usual spot. Our usual spot— she likes it too. A sickly, nervous smile twitches across her face. It must look exactly like the smile I'm wearing.

"Hey." She grabs the pole near my seat. The bus is pretty full, so she stands.

I pull out my earbuds. "Hey." She's streaked her hair with pink. It matches her fun-fur scarf perfectly. She brightens up the cold, dark day. "So, pink, huh?" is how the thought comes out of my mouth.

"Yeah." Sandra shrugs. She looks shy—kind of miserable.

"Looks good," I say.

She makes a face. "Yeah right." She looks through the window behind me.

I gaze out the window across the aisle. This is going to be a long ride.

I try to imagine the rumbling bus is really a massage chair, like they have on the top floor of the mall. I've put in my coins. I'm relaxing against the knobs as they churn up and down my spine.

In the bus seat next to me, there's a toddler on his mother's lap, but now she's stuffing him into the stroller—the one I almost fell on. He's not too happy about it—until he spots Sandra's scarf dangling above him.

He makes a few grabs for it. Sandra gives him a jokey, *back off* look, with flaring nostrils and buggy eyes. The kid doesn't even notice, he's so into the scarf. The mom's busy tapping on her phone. He strains against his seat belt and succeeds in grasping the scarf. Sandra's face galvanizes in fake horror as she tugs back.

This is better than the Three Stooges. The kid is laughing—*I'm* laughing—when the bus lurches to a hard stop. Sandra topples—she can't steady herself with the stroller pressing her knees like that. She's going to tip right onto the kid.

I reach out with both hands. Flailing, she manages to grab at me. I hold firm as she pulls herself upright again.

"Thanks." Sandra smiles at me—a real smile. *Wow.* It feels good to bask in that glow. Has it been that long? "I mean, thanks for asking me to join the act again," she explains.

Ah! That. She doesn't need to know I didn't vote one way or the other. I'm glad she's back now.

"After the way I walked off, I would have understood if you guys ditched me. That was so unprofessional..." Sandra's voice trails.

"Look, there are free seats in the back," I tell her. "We'll go sit there. This driver is a maniac."

"No, you get motion sickness," Sandra says.

"It's only a couple more stops. I'll be fine." I start to get up, but Sandra presses my shoulder back down.

"It's better here," she assures me.

We argue it out for the rest of the trip.

Twenty

The rec room at Seth and Jill's place is now stuffy and rank. I've almost passed out from all our practicing. I'm rolling a cold can of lemonade across my forehead. I would heave myself up to slide open the little basement windows—get some air in here—but my muscles are quivering like jelly.

Jill is squatting, pressing her elbow into the charley horse on Sandra's calf.

"Ow, ow, ow." Sandra's reaching my way, half laughing, half crying. "Save me," she moans.

Jill keeps pressing down, biting her lip in concentration.

"It gets rid of the cramp fast," Sofia assures Sandra. Sofia's bad foot is resting high in the old recliner chair. Her walking cast lies nearby, like a rejected bit of storm trooper.

Her leg finally released, Sandra curls up as if she wants to cradle it. "How about yours?" She nods at Sofia's foot, ensconced in a long white athletic sock.

"Six weeks, they figure." Sofia shrugs, taking a swill of her lemonade. "Then I can start physiotherapy."

Dawn's looking down on us all, hands on hips. "Sofia knows what it'll take to get back on both feet." She manages to make it sound like a lesson for the rest of us. She still isn't happy with the act just before Sandra's bit. "Instead of doing the monster stomp in sync, let's get the front row to come in late."

"Keep it simple, you always say!" Seth is spread-eagled on the vinyl tiles. But then he springs up into a front-back step, gaining speed and bounce. He throws himself down for his helicopter move—leg spinning in one direction, then the other, fast and easy. His practicing has paid off.

"Simple, yes, but not moronic. C'mon, it'll look good," Dawn insists.

With groans, the rest of us gather in formation. We face Sofia, our audience. Dawn and Sandra are in front. Seth, Jill and I are in a row behind. This kick-stomp move is somehow both gangster and Riverdance. I love it because it makes a ton of noise and gets out my aggression.

In the back row, we lead, just as we've been practicing. With Dawn's idea, she and Sandra must start a few beats later. When we get it, the rhythm sounds supercool. Now it's like Brazilian gangster meets Irish clog dancer. Sofia is actually clapping along, so it must be as good as I think.

"Okay, that's nice," Dawn announces. I should study her people skills. No one seems to mind when she bosses them. "Sandra, now you go forward for the big finale—" She shakes her head as Sandra moves. "You're not *working* it." Dawn turns to Sofia. "Hello? A little help?"

Jill, Seth and I fall back. Jill slouches, biting her thumb as Sofia and Dawn confer. Seth moves to the speakers. He replays his new mix of Donna Summer and the DMX tune. I bet he's listening for last-minute tweaks he might make. I creep back to my spot on the couch.

Sofia is now sitting up, making sinuous shapes in the air with her dancer arms. Sandra imitates, with Dawn helping adjust her pose here and there.

"Show her the butt strut," Sofia urges Dawn.

Me, I'm just enjoying the sight of Sandra being coached by the Donnas in a sexy sashay. I never would've dreamed it.

Isn't it cool when life comes up with better stuff than you ever imagined?

But wait—wow—Sandra is *slammin'*. Her hips are swiveling forward. Her shoulders shimmy back. Sandra looks...she looks...

"You're totally smoking hot," Dawn declares. She and Sofia exchange a satisfied nod. Sandra is blushing as she returns Dawn's high five.

"This may be our best Fashion Show yet," Jill muses.

Twenty-One

We're back in costume, waiting behind the curtain again.

This time, Seth has slicked his hair straight back. His eyes twinkle at me through rings of smudgy makeup. My eyes must be glowing back at him, even in this dim light. Jill did our makeup. We look excellent.

We all hung out late last night to keep Seth and Jill company while they made miniskirts out of Willow's tunic for the Franken-monsters. So even though we have different costumes, the gold theme connects us as a team. I take deep breaths, trying to calm my jitters. I can't believe we did it. I can't believe we're here. We're up next.

I turn around and whisper in Sandra's ear, "You look good." Along with the tunic and smudgy eyes, Sandra has her long hair done in a high ponytail. It juts out with this big Nefertiti-style hair clasp. Sandra knows how to style herself. She looks like a disco goddess.

I'm surprised how Dev's advice has really worked out. This has been so much more fun than our other act. We've all been listening to everyone's ideas, letting things fall apart, laughing together.

Plus, being off turbo mode has another bonus—I end up enjoying my friends better. And based on Sandra's smile shining on me right now, I'd say the feeling is mutual.

"Here." I twist a finger-curl into the end of her ponytail. "Now you're perfect." I'm totally satisfied with Sandra's finished look. Don't you love how sometimes when you step back, you can see so much better?

I smooth out my own tunic. It glows in the backstage gloom. As I mentally pat myself on the back for picking the right fabric, Sandra gets her wicked glint and says, "Who needs perfect? We got mad talent and personality, yo."

I can feel my face split into a grin. I'd throw myself on Sandra and give her a bear hug—but our act is *on*!

As we rush onstage, I remember how I almost quit. Was I nuts? How could I give up the chance to feel like this? It's like when we perform in the orchestra and in our bands and our choirs. It's like when we put on school plays. Fashion Show is an amazing combination of the best bits of everything!

The sound guy starts our music. Seth is rapt, listening to his own intro. He better snap out of it when it's time to start dancing. We hold position in two separate groups—backup singers and monsters—while the music samples chase each other in and out of the mix.

On the repeat, the peppy "Bad Girls" remix takes over, and we backup singers come to life. Sandra, Seth and I take turns doing a signature disco move, then freeze in position. When the rap comes in, Dawn and Jill do the same with a monster move each. This way we are establishing the two contrasting groups and their conflict. I glance at the judges' table. Our drama teacher is making a note on her paper. Our new act, Monster Disco Ball, has begun.

Sandra, Seth and I start with our backup-singer intro. But soon we're interrupted by Jill and Dawn, stomping across our sight line. We pose, all angry, and turn on our flashlights the way we used to do with Seth. The Franken-monsters perform their electric-zap moves—standing this time—and we click the flashlights off and on. In the strobe effect, their teased-up, Bride of Frankenstein hair wobbles. Their skirts twitch. The music fades back to Donna Summer, and they freeze as Seth slides, twists and moon-walks around them.

Then we work in a bit that Dawn insisted we slave over, back in the rec room. Sandra and I get tangled up in the powered-off monsters, trying to follow Seth as his backup singers. The judges are smiling. Their heads are moving to the music.

Now Jill and Dawn have returned to life, and the five of us square off. Seth catches Jill, and her heavy combat boot rises high, then swings down as she's pushed to one side. I fall against Dawn, and we do the same move. Pretty soon we're dancing together, passing the flashlights.

For my routine, I throw my head back and my arms out. Dawn and Jill lift me, moving me forward. At this point in the song there are only keyboards, playing the bass line. So it works that

I mimic some of the monster moves with Dawn and Jill before they fall back.

As I'm doing my full spin, a crack of light flashes from the auditorium doors. Someone enters. I see shadowy figures move among the seats. I fling my arms high and smile, as if I'm a star. We have the judges. I can see it in their eyes. The act is working.

Dawn is amazing. She's always spot on her mark. Jill's moves are tight, as if she's channeling Sofia's dancer spirit. Seth has been holding the beat for the rest of us since the beginning. He's like a metronome—nobody gets lost watching him. And Sandra, now at the foot of the runway, starts singing for real.

Her powerful voice needs no microphone. It fills the auditorium, all the way to the back row of the balcony. The music ends, but, according to plan, Sandra continues singing for several bars. The rest of us do one last turn, then stop—at the exact moment that Sandra goes quiet. As agreed, we all hold perfectly still in our poses for a four-count to finish.

Clapping and screaming erupt from the seats. The shadowy figures are clear now. There's Willow, jumping up and down. And Dev—giving us a standing ovation. His ear-splitting whistles bounce off the walls. Sofia's leaning on him, whooping and shouting, "Bravo! Encore!"

Their swell of appreciation washes toward us, lifting me up. Another swell, coming from my heart, makes me feel like I'll burst. Like Donna Summer says in the song, I feel love.

The judges are shaking their heads at all the racket, but they're smiling. "Thanks very much, ah…" Our drama teacher checks her notes. "…Monster Disco Ball. That was terrific."

I reach out for the others—we're all reaching. And in one swoop, in perfect unison, we take our bow.

Author's Note

Adina's story is inspired by FACE School, located in the heart of downtown Montreal. FACE stands for Fine Arts Core Education (although according to graffiti in the girls' bathroom, it stands for Fun, Action, Creation, Énergie).

My children have attended the school for years. Like Adina and her friends, the students of FACE dash between classes, carrying bulging backpacks, rushing up and down a coiling, M.C. Escher-style staircase. The medieval-looking basement and the ex-swimming-pool performance space are the same too. Intergrade activities such as reading partners, pen pals and "family" classes help create connections between senior students and little ones.

While less polished than the musical concerts FACE students perform several times a year, the popular student-led Fashion Show offers a unique party buzz. Audiences pack to the back of the balcony—hooting and cheering over a two-hour show of big ensemble numbers.

My thanks go to my children and their friends and teachers, who for all these years—unbeknownst to them and me—have been providing the background and inspiration for *Show Mode*. My son's buddy, Matthew Williams, and his violin teacher, Kate Bevan-Baker, allowed me to observe a lesson, answering my foolish questions with grace. Fellow FACE mom—and good friend—Abha Joshi kindly read the story for any egregious errors in South Asian references. Ninaad Kalla, a member of the FACE 2016 graduating class, read the story with an eye toward music-related blunders. I'm grateful to all these kind advisors. Any mistakes in the book are mine.

The author of four books for children, RAQUEL RIVERA has lived and worked in Washington D.C., Kuala Lumpur, Singapore, Barcelona and Toronto (where she was born and raised). She now lives in Montreal, Quebec, with her family. For more information, visit www.raquelriverawashere.com.

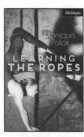